Author's Preface

This book is David's story and mine. We became inseparably linked by our dying to true belief as imparted to us both in harmful ways by people who thought themselves well-intentioned. Throughout our ministry to each other, I would learn how it's possible that suffering that is not my own could affect me as though it were my own and with such force that it could move me forward beyond my spiritual inertia. Our friendship was not a matter of reason—one person helping another. There was nothing reasonable about setting our lives in clear danger for the other if we were only superficial friends. I sense we saw each other for the first time, having nothing more in mind than recognizing that we both were in need and peril for our life and soul. Life would never be whole until it was taken up in another's life.

People of faith should be the last to falsify their lives. Truthfulness is important not only for the sake of honesty, but because there is a connection between the truth of God and the truth of a life, even a battered life like David's, in which the grace of God is ultimately disclosed.

There is a rawness within these pages—coarse language, hints of blasphemy, and spiritual violence directed toward David. As a minister, I have tried not to preach or go soft-focus at the hard parts. There is much in this memoir that is not pretty. The divide between David and his parents was inescapable, and there is a pronounced incompleteness to the work. Writing is like confessing, except that it is harder and almost never followed by absolution. There is no resolution chapter; there is only the hope that in life we sometimes need better friends.

The thought of altering the truth to appease concerned parties, or speaking the truth in spite of potential chaos, seem unacceptable sacrifices. Despite my attempts, David's parents refused to respond to my requests to share their story, their reflections after these ten years since David's death. For that reason, the names of the major characters have been changed at the suggestion of the publisher. The dialogue has been re-created from David's journal and my memory of our multiple conversations.

I offer my profound thanks to those who walked with us on our journey, offering needed perspective and gracious love. They know who they are. To my niece, Amber Moody Stuart, your cover artwork, so beautiful and haunting, represents our walk of faith through the deep valley, even as we looked to the hills.

Contents

Introduction: *Considering the Wilderness*

Chapter One: *Approaching the Wilderness*

Chapter Two: *A Wilderness Challenge: Letting Go of First Faith*

Chapter Three: *Something or Someone Has to Die*

Chapter Four: *Moving Forward Incrementally*

Chapter Five: *The Danger of Shrines*

Chapter Six: *The Darkness is a Map*

Chapter Seven: *The Stranglehold of Preconditions*

Chapter Eight: *Imagining God Differently*

Chapter Nine: *Finding Better Friends*

Chapter Ten: *The Wilderness is an Acceptable Graveyard*

Chapter Eleven: *Protecting God*

Chapter Twelve: *Purging Faith's Destructiveness*

Chapter Thirteen: *Humility Before God is an Option*

Chapter Fourteen: *Story is More Important than Theology*

Chapter Fifteen: *Our Justice and God's Justice*

Chapter Sixteen: *Hypocrisy Has Its Merits*

Chapter Seventeen: *Who Will Win the Memorial Service*

Epilogue: *Resolution is Often Solitary*

Introduction

Considering the Wilderness

What is the writer trying to do for himself or herself by writing? Not as a writer, but as a person.
Kenneth Burke

Every religion possesses the capacity to be true when thought of metaphorically. Religion finds trouble when metaphors become facts, when people rest too comfortably in the perceived truth of their scriptures' historical integrity. Metaphors take us places beyond the cells of our religious assurances imprisoned in our creeds, doctrines, traditions, bedtime stories, and prayers. They prod and poke us to the point of irritation, away from other chains and toward unimagined connections with people.

Metaphors introduced me to people like David, whose relationship with me was established first as an overture to responsible faith action. Along the way, our relationship became prominent, winning most days and certainly my best life.

I first met David in the spring of 2006, a few days into the strangest Lenten season I can remember. In retrospect, I had not planned on giving up that much for Lent. I had not considered taking up a new passion. Before my introduction to David, I knew myself only as a spiritual representative of a church that appeared to selective outside observers to be on the right side of justice. I remember it as a fulfilling gig, despite time's insistent demand for a more careful appraisal. My spiritual path, almost imperceptibly, became a rut, a tranquil, nourishing rut, true, even educational, but a rut nonetheless. Its strength? It offered little harm and much good, but it became a spiritual wheel stuck in a ditch. As I learned more about David's spiritual victimization, however, I felt an overpowering urge to steer in the direction of healing. My problem? I never reflected to see what kind of healer I might be, or even if I should consider such a designation. I knew only I was weary of the spiritual violence being exercised and exacerbated in my town by people of faith, bullies really, who offered no quarter and were quick to divide the teams. I let myself dream that the church's ministry to David was a promising battle to fight. That's how it is with dreams. They're the perfect crime.

I missed that most faith battles are violent battles. Covenant United Church of Christ, the church I served for twelve years, possessed a built-in sense of justice. Founded on anti-slavery in 1834, our justice history became the church's only remembered history. Teams from the church traveled to the South to register voters in the 1960s. Having only a vague understanding of eternal life, they put themselves in comfortable danger for the right to add an addendum—eternal life is at least the life where all share in humanity's best possibilities. The church championed women's rights in the 1980s. They did the hard work to learn about gay rights and how to welcome the LGBTQ community, voting in 2008 to become an Open and Affirming Congregation.

The church faced what we proudly recognized as persecution for our commitment to justice. Protestors held vigils outside the church, offended by our inclusive Halloween party for our LGBTQ friends. Scripture placards, foisted high enough for easy reading by passersby, their letters in a high block, particularly offensive Calabria font, highlighted the selective verses in the Bible supporting their opposing views on homosexuality. We voted to be embarrassed for them and their interpretive incompetence.

What shall we do with evil, the Apostle Paul throws out in Romans 12. We hated it. We hated cruelty, arrogance, and greed, violence, the outrages of war, the abuse of children; hated that millions die of hunger and disease that might have been prevented; hated racism and prejudice of every kind; hated the desecration of the earth; hated the epidemic degradation of sex; hated all slander and lies; hated the mean and thoughtless words spoken to each other; hated our ungodly indifference to the suffering all around us; hated the people who were irksome, immature, rude, or just wrong, the people who were dismissive of us, or said terrible things to us, or about us; hated the people who opposed or undermined what we believed in, the people we felt betrayed us, and the ones who broke our hearts.

And occasionally, we forgot to loosen our grip on our first and most strident presupposition: We knew and understood perfect justice. Justice became a cavalier idol. We did not allow enough space to approach justice with a sense of our own ignorance. We rested sleepily in our proper and just assumptions; and we played the justice card without realizing it cut off all debate with those who opposed David. Any effort toward their possible rehabilitation or reintegration was not worth the risk or heartache. There were limits to what malevolence we were willing to bear. We stood on what we assumed were inviolate scruples.

When the Hebrews eventually stood in the Promised Land, Canaan's "fair and happy land," after forty years, they choked out the words, "We have known abundance." I don't doubt their veracity, but I am suspicious if the words would have been uttered without their wilderness, without their experiencing a proper wasteland, and without their opposing God who continued to lead them through the wilderness, toppling golden calves along their circuitous route with the frequency and efficiency of teenagers leveling mailboxes with Louisville Sluggers as after-prom mischief.

The wilderness exposes as little else does. For all the beauty of the earth, its glens and dales and valleys, bluffs and mesas, mountain vistas and water spouts, it offers dozens of hideouts for idols. Not so in the wilderness. In the wilderness, idols can only sit on sand under a barren sky. In the wilderness, idols are exposed. We idolize our best life, what we have always assumed as right, as just, pining for its affirming stroke across our cheeks, while neglecting to consider just how empty of God it might be. Our wilderness seasons do not create the cancer that comes out of us; they expose what was already there. It is in the wilderness, ironically, that we witness one of God's great kindnesses: Putting our idols in plain view so that we might see them, hate them, maybe for the first time, and eventually give them a desert grave.

As we ministered to David, we faced a kind of evil at work, and it stirred a kind of evil in me. Anger became my first friend, perhaps my only friend. I looked at our named opponents with contempt, even as I tried to keep it hidden. I wanted to stop the perpetuation of violence toward David but failed to realize my oneness with his opponents. I never considered how deep my smugness, my scorn toward those whose understanding of God seemed so ineffectual and how they were themselves forms of violence. I wanted to end the violence but was going about it with violence in my heart. I opposed those who did evil with anger, forgetting the evil I had embraced. The Buddhists speak of the safety of the soul. It can be a point of release if I recognize that others have all the goodness I have, and, conversely, that I have the same capacity for evil as those whose actions I abhor.

After naming evil as a reality, Paul adds another more disturbing phrase, *"do not repay anyone evil for evil,"* (Romans 12:17) and that we are to *"overcome evil with good,"* (Romans 12:21). Sounds good in theory. In practice, not so much. Overcome evil with good? What does that mean? I sense it requires I start by snuffing out the cycle of evil where I am. The nature of evil is to recreate itself and multiply itself by how I respond to it. I am enraged and I hurt someone else, provoking their rage, so they hurt me, provoking my rage, and I hurt them, and the cycle goes on, and not just between us. It spins itself out to others around us, who then spin out on their own. Back and forth it goes, lives are diminished or destroyed, and a world is in flames. W.H. Auden said it simply enough: "I and the public know what the schoolchildren learn, those to whom evil is done, do evil in return."

The perpetuation of spiritual violence will never end unless enough people find a way of saying, "It stops here, we're done; let's have something new." Somebody has to break the cycle. I wanted it to be me. Somebody has to absorb what's been dished out so far. I hoped I would consider it. Somebody has to offer some alternative of love. I wept that it would not be me.

I never get to decide what others will do or refuse to do. Paul is realistic about this. Just after saying, *do not repay evil for evil,* (Romans 12:17) Paul says, *if it is possible, so long as it depends on you, live peaceably with all* (Romans 12:18). I take responsibility for my part, and that is all. As long as it depends on me, I must choose love's gestures, words, and silences with humility and prayer.

I learned about these possibilities in the wilderness, as a hundred burning bushes in the canyon of my mind. They presented first as a threat, cultivating in my life that one quality so beneficial to living faith: desperation. Left to myself in undisturbed certainty, I will always wander, careless with that one part of me I cannot afford to lose: my soul. In the wilderness, I do not have the luxury of indifference. When I am desperate, I find that I can scarcely go through an hour, much less a day, without lifting my heart in confession for all the ways I have insisted I must be right. It would be in the wasteland where I found membership in that great company of the poor in spirit who believed God draws near brokenness, too often self-inflicted, who sensed that compared to a godless promised land, a God-filled wilderness is a heaven.

Years of one sort of turmoil or another had rubbed my spirit until it was as raw as the rug burns administered by my older brothers when we wrestled as children. I've been healed to the degree that I am tranquil, a calm revealed within and without. The wilderness has been my residence for more days than I care to admit. Thankfully, it now serves only as an entry point, never as my permanent lodging. The wilderness smoothed the frayed edges, leaving me longing, not for the perfect but the complete. There was something incomplete about my spiritual walk. I dedicated my ministry to the avoidance of the treacherous trails and ravines that are part of any soul's landscape. How silly of me, piloting my ship in a slip-shod fashion and then be shockingly surprised at what an inappropriate port I found myself docked.

There is a sense in which awareness can be as stagnating as laziness. The song, "Let There Be Peace on Earth," ends with a chilling phrase: "And let it begin in me." There was a time when I thought it was an inane sentiment, maybe a little too self-important, that peace on earth might begin with me. I don't find it silly anymore. When I say no to continuing the cycle of hatred and hurt, God's peace has a chance where I am—and love may spark its own cycles. This is God's way of changing the world and me. I have seen it in Christ—God refusing to answer evil with evil, but overcoming evil with love. And how powerfully it may still work in me. And God is forever looking for accomplices.

I remember the accomplices in my journey of memories, remembrances of women and men who, unbeknownst to them, learned to teach death some manners. I will forever defend their integrity. They rarely imitated the low behavior of David's parents and their early band of followers. They were gentle most days when others were rough, polite when others were uncouth. You will read their names in these pages: Lara, Evie, William, Ruth, Camille and Jack. You may be drawn to them in these pages, some image of them, their physical traits; you may form ideas about their strengths and their weaknesses, but you will never know completely the depth of their hearts and good minds.

I thrashed in the clear waters of their wisdom pooling near my heart. I managed to dirty the waters for these dear friends, but somehow, miraculously even, they knew better than I how to beat back hypocrisy. They responded effectively, not perfectly, with mercy and kindness toward those who did evil toward our David. They met hostility and irritation with enough peace that evil was redeemed every other day.

I am forever grateful. Envious, but grateful.

Chapter One

Approaching the Wilderness

If we really want to live, we'd better start at once to try; if we don't, it doesn't matter, but we'd better start to die. W.H. Auden

A man, late thirties, dressed practically in button-down comfort, bounded up the left side of the church's two stairwells. His stride defiant; his casual wingtips nipped his khakis and landed with such force the solemn air under his shoes dissipated to the corner of the first landing. His physical presence and demeanor requested your attention and curiosity, a man whose mind greatly needed independence but on which nothing substantial long imposed itself.

He brushed by the usher standing at the top of the stairs meekly distributing wilted memorial bulletins, damp in his hands from the July humidity, to "catholic for a day" contestants playing with votive fire just inside the Protestant vestibule.

"Yankee candles in a makeshift candelabrum fashioned from a Boy Scout Court of Honor," one member shared smiling. "It fits us. It's tacky, but it fits."

"We have work to do," the man mumbled, pushing past the gathered mourners. He stood anxiously, his frame resting against the west wall, and appearing to those of us who would later revise our more favorable initial impressions as a grifter looking for his next mark. Above his head, three stained glass windows, presented to the congregation by their anti-slavery friends in the 1850s for their early abolitionist efforts, served as sentinels over the proceedings. The sun broke through the windows in soft blue, their one-o'clock color, highlighting the frumpled robe of the black Good Shepherd pulling stray lambs toward an unknown fold.

He scouted the sanctuary that, when described by the historical society, read like a real estate brochure. The room was large, brown ceilings and walls, and dusky corners, a vernacular adaptation to the decorative style of principles of late Gothic architecture--bends and twists, stamped florets and foliated fleur-de-lis, buttresses and hood molds, and lancet windows. The soft light poured in and shaded points of emphasis, and the deep greenness in the outside courtyard always seemed to be peeping in and emitting well-ordered privacy. According to agents, the room showed well.

The man checked himself with the thought of hundreds of people in the room who were less sure than himself. In the front left corner of the sanctuary he saw fierce friends, huddled, men and women who, like him, found comfort in using Jesus as an imaginary friend, people who were in the habit of taking for granted, on scanty evidence, that they were right. Their errors and delusions, a web of vague outlines, had never been checked by the judgment of people speaking as an opposing authority. We were never introduced. I learned later that he served as the teacher at Genoa Church of Christ, the home church of David's parents, Peter and Nora.

Both sides, those who loved David and those who despised him, held in our hands a necessary component for healing: the assembly of persons broken hearted and stunned by grief. The afternoon memorial played out differently, "every third thought our grave." I assumed too much; I put aside warnings from dear friends. Forced into the same space, both sides managed only the spectacular avoidance of despisement. We refused any redirection of judgment, and seeing each other was the final act of putting faces to hatred.

There is a coronation of every soul, a celebration open to all. As we live, we invite whom we will and exclude whom we will. We were offended by their presence, by what we imagined them to look like—dour men, protectors of the faith, apologists searching for an audience; and women, frumpy in comfortable shoes, whose theology matched their hairstyles—straight without the benefit of a gentle curl. I imagined them in my mind as people with enough pieces of the cross to build an ark.

Covenant Church refused to wallow in their postulates, faith rules that appeared as deceptive as they were enticing. We assigned them to the spiritually dead and let them bury themselves. Our temple, now encumbered with money changers, printed unspoken burial notices in our hearts.

"Why are they here?" a long-time member of the church asked. "Why can't they let David rest. They didn't give a shit about him, and now they are the grieving family. A receiving line for God's sake. That's brazen. I'd respect them more if they stayed away."

"Let's try and find the least objectionable way to offer kindness," I said.

"There are water and glasses near the casket, a box of tissues and a chair," he said. "That's about all the kindness I can stomach. Anything more, they need to ask."

A center arch dominated the chancel. It was there that we put David. In that space, pacing in front of the casket, we played out theological segregation, both sides using the Bible as a personal crutch--literalists to the right and those who grew weary of searching for theological loopholes to the left. "We have work to do," he had said. For the briefest of moments, I entertained the idea that "his work, their work," might include confession, even a brief acknowledgment that they could have treated David better. I even let myself imagine choking out absolution without spitting up.

The Genoa representatives convened in the sanctuary corner next to the church's grand piano, an irony not lost to those of us who knew the church's refusal to incorporate musical instruments in their worship services. Their teacher, Ron Porter, repositioned the ranks, the strongest men stationed at the head of David' casket wearing contempt as a lapel flower. He beat back any doubt that their treatment of David was not faithfulness to the God they served and the book they worshipped. We gathered to celebrate David's life with us. They viewed the service as a blasphemous recognition of a reprobate.

I stood in the front of the sanctuary with my arms folded, wearing presumption as my spiritual tattoo, and forgetting just how difficult originality is in everything that matters most. How heavily influenced I have been by those who first preserved and reserved a faith for me. I remember their insistence, what they assumed was their gift to me. And on this day of remembering our dead friend, I watched a similar, defiant oligarchy.

"We did the right thing," Evie said, a woman a little too firm perhaps in her graver moments, but who possessed an enchanting range of concession. She assured me the Sunday after David's service that "It was what he wanted, what he made us promise."

"Who came up with the table and place setting next to the casket?" I asked.

"Ruth," Evie said. "No cookie-cutter funeral for our David. We throw a great funeral. He loved serving our Hot Meal guests dinner. Good china, silverware, cloth napkins, and no Styrofoam."

"Nice touch. Great faith symbol—everyone included at the table. It worked. Everything worked. Even the open casket worked. Brought back some disturbing memories in my first church, but it worked," I said.

"David said he wanted an open casket because it would be the last time he would be on stage," Evie laughed.

"The last time he would be the center of attention," I added. "Still can't figure out how a gay man with AIDS conned a priest out of a Catholic cemetery plot."

"He was a charmer," she said.

"Some might say a manipulator," I said, smiling.

Evie paused. "That he was." She then looked too hard at me. Tears puddled in the corner of her eyes, her face revealing everything that we had just shared was a preface for what she wanted to say. "We didn't change any hearts."

"Is that what we were going for, trying to change the hearts of the Pryns and their minions?" slightly irritated at her implication that we missed something important.

"I don't know," she said. "I guess I was hoping. I mean, we held all the cards--our church, our minister. Jesus, we paid for the funeral! We made sure the only message that would get out was our love for David. Your message hit all the right points about inclusion. Anyone attending the service would know where our church stands. But I hoped for more."

"From the Pryns? Their church?" I asked incredulously. "They stood at David's head. We hung around his feet. David lying dead in the middle, the reason for separation. And they stood there peddling their faith as cast iron. Not one tear from David's parents. Not one. Nothing. But to be fair to them, I didn't expect anything, not after what I saw the night he died."

"We managed the room," she pushed. "And we put the service in the Pryns' faces."

"Deservedly so," I said.

"We created caricatures. We made them up," she countered. "They were exactly what we needed them to be. We never got the whole story. We got David's story. That's all."

"We didn't make them up," I said. "They professed in letters and refusals their commitment to deny any blessing toward David. I did let myself hope for some moment that we might weep together, but they were not going to let that happen. And, if I am honest, not many in the room wanted it to happen. The Pryns and their lot were their own Abraham. They needed an Isaac to sacrifice. So, they took David and laid him out. And they plunged the knife, deaf to any late entry from God. We didn't make them up."

Sometimes initial observations play out as true, or what we want to be true. From the earliest biblical story of Adam and Eve and their expulsion from the bliss of Eden, a starting point is chosen and people spend their lives searching for whatever it is that validates that first choice. The path is set before us, and the first few steps or climbs, we assume, will determine the beauty of the walk or its fright. As life is lived, as we experience its intrusion, any reconsideration of the initial path is wrought with fear because we can't bear the thought that our beginning assumption about God might be flawed.

I find it sobering that each side who walked near David began a journey that, at its inception, was essentially the same journey because we were searching for some idea of God. Each of us had to say what we were searching for, and what was revealed was there would be as many answers as there were searches. But would there be general answers that would serve to the benefit of all? Both sides searched for safety and affirmation found in groupings, people to love and love us; both sides even found significant work to do. Even as we found these things, something crucial was missing which, sadly, neither side found.

Covenant Church began its search for the only idea of God worth keeping, as did the Genoa Church of Christ. Two different searches for God, two different doors opening to a path marked with nothing but sky and mystery. I confess I gladly preferred to let the other side walk alone, choosing only to interact with them in sporadic skirmishes. And what I have to say about those who opposed David has little to do with my currently fashionable memory revisions.

Faith is often crippled by its own purity, as well as by the people who express it. I championed a cause without knowing the cause perfectly or completely. I chained faith and surrendered it to a softer legalistic rigorism; I turned God into a kinder witch with a gingerbread fetish. I side-stepped my named enemies and shuffled near them with a healthy dose of suspicion for three years. They viewed David only as an earthly imperfection which easily and effortlessly became his sinfulness. To eradicate it was interpreted by them as a pious act.

God's creation is good until it meets with the ambiguities of its own goodness. God is never who people would be if they were God. Infinite purity calls us to find our place among the sinners who live next door in our hearts. We began our journey with David and with each other, our backpacks stuffed with the "things we chose to carry." It became our institution. David seemed to know better, resting in the belief of his ultimate inseparability from God. Instead of just seeking God or the unknown elements in his soul, he sensed that the day, every day, "the unknown seeks the known." This recognition did not heal his essential wound, his aloneness and abandonment, but he spent fewer hours beating his head and heart against it. He learned the people who said "no" had been saying nothing all along.

To have faith is to be set free from any false conceptions of God. God can never serve as the missing link to boast about or justify our loudest expressions of religiosities. To be certain of faith is relatively easy if God is reduced to the convenient attributes of a blind idol. It is more difficult to be sure of one's sight, one's faith, when one is confronted by God through the debility of one's existence.

These days I cringe that at one point in my life I walked side by side next to the Pryns, our stories blending inconsistently, and me carrying a pocketful of rocks in the alb I refused to wear in Sunday worship. I carried my personal vile of poison, awaiting my chance to poison the meal they chose to sit down to—suspicion and distrust, the second or third cousins to spiritual deformation. I have learned these past years that I cannot walk too long harboring no contempt or repugnance toward them and their distortion of love. The Pryns appeared to know where to look for grace, in the cupboards of their making. David felt at ease waiting for grace's surprise, that the right place and time are never to be found in the future, or in any withdrawal from the world, and never to be found in a separatist community.

How deadly the path of self-deification, absorbed early, and brought to fruition as easily as one sits down to a favorite spiritual buffet—a side of feathery flagellation and a dollop of bitter justification. Self-deification has no advisor to moderate the temptation to spiritual criminality of trying to correct nature left imperfect. How limiting are the tools packed for first spiritual trips to achieve one's distorted and unexamined ends.

The Pryn's son was gay, and it became an unbearable imperfection for them. They lived and acted in ways to remove it with a surgeon's scalpel without offering David the benefit of anesthesia. David never submitted; he refused to sacrifice who he was created to be in order to fulfill his parents' delusions of deity. His deeper search consisted in recognizing the incompatibility of religious-like pretensions of perfection and the character of his God.

Chapter Two

A Wilderness Challenge: Letting Go of First Faith

I have to ask myself, am I disenchanted by religion or the counterfeit of it? John Donne

I grew up believing sin as the worst that I do, but the heartbreaking truth is sin is always insinuating itself into the best that I do and the holiest I know. To consider faith is to learn the dance of contradictions. I am kind and insensitive, gracious, and harsh. I am not stupid, living under the weight of ignorance or dreariness, but I am mean too many days. I want to be good and virtuous while at the same time wanting people to know how good and virtuous I am. I live as a collection of inconsistencies, the most deceptive and imperceptible being believing the weakness in me that masks as divinity, the creation of my own myth.

I would have written David's story differently ten years ago, at that fractured time in my life when I believed righteous anger could serve as faith and granting me the license to be permanently incensed. I had yet to examine how muddled is the distinction between genuine outrage and feigned righteousness. I needed a foil, an antagonist. I needed Nora Pryn and to imagine her only as a rumor. She represented the tragic part of happiness I wanted for David, his right to see God differently made wrong by someone else.

Faith has served me well; a fine idol polished to a bowling trophy sheen, its charm buried in the gathered dust beneath the base of my certainties about God. It moves slowly at times, at the speed to which I live my life. I have never been afraid of faith, but I have lived my life fearful of failing in faith. It has become my doctrine of fine linen, valuable only because I have lived my life too carefully; its value reduced with each spill and stain. It hovers over me as pain, as truth, truth too intolerable to bear at times. But my pain, its internalization, serves now as the authentic origin of my spiritual memory, and I have no idea how much consolation I will require.

My time with David was the way meaning got started. I watched his tortured life play out. I assisted in the storm blowing against his light. I tried to protect him from those who buffeted against him, the ones who refused to give him what he needed most--a good death. In the end, it was all he had. There would be days when those of us who ministered to him daily would struggle to remember why we did, but David was never so passionate than when he commanded us to go on living to ensure that he did not bear a wounded name.

The idea of him living on in our memories, that paltry piece of immortality, felt hollow to David, but it was all he could muster. I sense David wanted what he accomplished in the last three years of his life remembered, but preferred to be around to enjoy it. He had long since rescued himself from modest claims and objectives. Why not go big?

He cared for his reputation as he died; his broken name, who would save it, clear it, his final anxiety. Given the number of people he so gratuitously used, and so often, especially early in what he described as his "prodigal" period, his concern seemed justified. We would serve as his scribes, his interpreters. He would have his way with all of us.

Despite the brutal treatment he inflicted on friends before we met him, we forgave him, minimized his prior life precisely and as quickly as we forgave ourselves. We learned to paint in muted colors when describing him, predisposed to looking for any soft landing on homosexual soil, and absolving him of prior missteps because he was gay. At first, we were an open and affirming group unable to consider that being an asshole is not a matter of sexual orientation.

As we lived and breathed David Pryn, however, we learned there was something far from dead in his heart and spirit, something ready or willing, a story beyond the weakness of the flesh.

I found myself singularly devoted to the perverse joy that his parents would never know the new faith horizon he envisioned. How quickly I learned my penchant for displeasing others, how cunning I was in my attempts to catch "proper saints," those who separated from him because of his sexual orientation. Depicting their harshness and spiritual violence proved more fun to write about than well-being and bliss. I possessed the memory of a battered dog and was chained to the conviction that righteous anger granted me spiritual immunity. I baited David's parents, finding my intention more cathartic than cruel, enacting for me the ritual expulsion of a scapegoat.

I confess I am no longer interested in fanning whatever embers of my judgment remain toward David's parents and their choir of friends, men and women, who sang in each other's ears the ugliest of hymns. Such is the seasonal strength of indignation, time wresting from me the power of significant outrage. And any confession insists I also acknowledge those forced into my orbit, my dearest friends. My lostness, once so consuming, found a home in their hearts. For that, I am ashamed and ask forgiveness.

Still, I feel no need to revise David's parents who served for me already the perfection of malign will and genius for despisement. My remembrance of that time is as acute as ever, but it is now much less satisfying. I don't hate them, but I cannot reconcile my heart to them. An offended mind, whatever else it may miss, is rarely in need of reasons. The Pryns claimed their truth so insistently--any lapse toward empathy grievous to them; a generosity of spirit to this one, their son, a poison. David died slowly by their unkindness. They presented to me as dark visions of human nature and far too accepting of the darkness. They seemed to be endlessly at war with someone, moral pyromaniacs ready to set any encounter ablaze.

    I don't like to think that I could ever grow fond of the Pryns, but I needed them as I watched David's life wither. They would serve as my appropriate chaos. Ours would be a war of religion, each side protecting their faith interpretations and playing out in front of everyone except upon the battlefields. I felt at the time of David's death that we were victorious. We saw his life through to the end. But looking back, what did we win? David was still dead and gloating, had a shelf life. We rested smugly in our sense of rightness, and our assurance that belief, when exposed as fraudulent, cannot be regenerated without additional deformity. We expected the Pryns to climb into the tomb of intransigent faith positions, nakedly exposed at David's memorial, and be forced to live whatever days they had left bitter that someone threatened and challenged their positions. The death of the Pryns' belief in their son became the birth of my invention. There should not be injustices, and I sought any means to destroy them. I warmed myself near the blaze of righteous anger, stoking the flame against those who espoused separation from David. It was not just the narrowness they prescribed; it was wrong.

    Whatever truthfulness I found these past ten years since David's passing comes from having my ego bruised and bloodied by my hypocrisy. I wished to hold fast to justice but found I felt most comfortable in petty revenge. The pleasure derived proved unfulfilling. It fed my bitterness, but I still was chained. I've spent my life incarnating the value of my personality while turning aside from the value of love, my character, merely a series of successful gestures and kindnesses. I live now trying to reconstruct the psychological and spiritual complexity from my hidden ruins, fearful that there can be no inner check on the soul when the soul is an abyss.

How preposterous to assume God needs my protection from people whose interpretation of scripture, I reasoned, was as shallow as the deepest puddle. It felt right to try, however. I dismissed the Pryns and justified my actions using partial evidence, hearsay, and careless perceptions. Any method of interpretation is dangerous because of the habit of details chosen and emphasized. I became the grandest of inquisitors; I became an equal oppressor.

Righteous anger requires little preliminary work. It needs only a villain, one whose story does not fit my understanding of God, faith, and unconditional love. In many ways, righteous anger is more motto than constitution. It presents nobly at first as a clarion call for immediate change; it is highly combustible in its charge and propels one forward into the mass that is one's choir. It is oblivious that the warning signs of any cause, regardless of its initial moral thrust, goads one, in the words of Shakespeare, "to sin in loving virtue."

How much of our faith journey is locked in fear? The surprising nature of God's welcome spooks us because we know people who merit our judgment. The side we choose, the favorite we gravitate toward, subverts God's indiscriminate love for all people without conditions, limits, or exceptions. It assumes God hates the enemies of my naming. According to Martin Neimoller, a German pastor who protested the anti-Semite measures in Nazi Germany, "It took me a long time to learn that God is not the enemy of my enemies. God is not even the enemy of God's enemies." What if faith has nothing to do with choosing sides? It has been my experience that faith is not as much fun. There is also the insecurity of resting in God, that God's promise of unconditional love means there is love enough for me. Reaching that point of discovery has proven problematic for me.

In Jesus' parable on the "Wheat and Weeds," the boss, when told that weeds have been planted among the wheat, sown by an enemy in the wee hours of the morning, replies, "No matter. Do not let that consume you. Let them grow together." The workers, the ones who have toiled in the sun to plant the best, are perplexed. The boss has his reasons, because in pulling up the weeds, they may pull up the wheat as well. "*Let both of them grow together,*" (Matthew 13:30) the boss instructs. *At the harvest, matters will be made right.*

It is often the nature of people of faith to assume "wheatiness." I assumed I was always more wheat, but I seemed to prefer living among the weeds. They were more fun. I now know I am both wheat and weed. I also know that when I am most like wheat, I am most vulnerable to the vicissitudes of judgment and accusation. When, without humility, if I am right, if I need to be right, I will choose as my first course to pull up the weeds around me, the ones who steal my sunlight, the ones who irritate me and threaten my ideology. My sense of rightness overtakes me.

What I missed for years is the nature of the enemy, that the enemy in the night has deliberately sown weeds among the wheat. He then leaves the field, the scene of the destruction, confident that the damage he intends will come to fruition. But how can he be so sure? I sense the enemy understands the nature of the wheat, the good folk. They will do his job for him. They will pull up the weeds and destroy the wheat as well. The enemy does not have to worry if his intent will be successful. It is a given—good folks becoming bad folks by trying to put bad folks out of business.

But what if justice is to name whatever is an insult to the God of love and mercy given to all—the weeds and wheat? That justice is to speak out, not because it hurts our hearts, but because it hurts God's heart. And how does such humility impact our sensibilities—how we conduct ourselves in our pursuit of the righteous path?

Righteous anger has its place. It is not just the purview of people of faith. I have witnessed the gallantry of dear friends standing in whatever breach presented to them, people who have never considered faith for legitimate reasons. But these days, these dangerous days, I continue to think and act from a perspective that fits me spiritually. My beginning assumptions are critical. I forget how often I slip in and out of faith. As a person who mentions faith regularly to my congregation, I still marvel at my inability to nail down this rabbi from Nazareth--this golden child of responsible righteous anger—sweeping his sacred space clean of charlatans making a buck off pre-packaged spiritual souvenirs, people preying on the superstitious and naïve, frightening them with threats that God required something more than simple piety.

Jesus' temple spat, more illustrative than a method, reveals the mechanics of righteous anger, how it finds expression—the number of folding chairs that must be thrown across a church fellowship hall to make a point. Missed in the cleansing of the temple is the number of people left in his wake. What we forget is his action in the temple was the exception to the way he normally confronted the rigidity of his religion and the tyranny of political power in his day. But then most faith journeys are primarily about exceptions. It is the marrow that strengthens our hypocrisy as followers. We dare not consider, even for the briefest of moments, the way he ultimately faced down the powers that be by seeing his ministry to the end without violence.

Jesus left the victims temporarily speechless until the furniture was restored to its perfect place, until the business people met in the parking lot after Sabbath. Something would have to be done with this rabbi. Even the stupidest of martyrs, they reasoned, would never have upset the communion table and altar chairs in the sanctuary.

What Jesus conveniently seems to ignore is the remnants of his outburst, those in the wake of his righteous anger. How is righteous anger to be expressed without adding to the already potent toxicity of the situation? He offers only the fitful prescription, recorded much earlier in his ministry, on a day when people were weary with the heat and the mountain too small to provide shade: "*Do not judge too harshly thinking that while you may have the upper hand, morally speaking, you are granted immunity from the same exacting judgment.*" I think I am not above having my motives questioned, no matter how sweet the taste of moral superiority.

Faith, even dressed up in its most elegant clothes, is subject to spotting. It is joyfully impure because I am impure. For most of my life, I have tried to possess faith as a talisman, hanging from my meager life by the cheapest of chains, that if worn daily, no matter the tarnishing, it will at least grant my death more sadness from the gathered mourners at my memorial.

Faith, I have learned, is best expressed as grace. It is a quiet noun, experienced as a verb. There are few rules. It doesn't play well with rules, except impermanence. My life plays out under "chronos" time and "kairos" time. They are both measures of time, but "chronos" time is how long my life plays out, while "kairos" time is about how my life plays out. I sense "kairos" time wants to win my life. It involves a choice; it is never subject to the vicissitudes of the length of days. We clothe ourselves from life's wardrobe of grace or defeat. To live under faith's soft shadow and inviting light is to find release, that my ugliest scars will be kissed with the saddest of tears of what might have been.

On his better days, David resigned himself as to how his life would eventually play out. The temptation to make his case to God faded into death's firm summons. He learned to trust God's unconditional love, the love he had shit on for ten years. He learned grace and extended it. He was also not above using self-pity to get his way. There were more times, however, when he looked like an innocent among the hungriest of scavengers, people circling his life to pick his bones and savoring whatever marrow of condemnation they could suck.

David resembled a twig in comfortable shoes. He was born with a perfect face, chiseled, ashen around keen eyes sunken to a manageable depth. His disease pinched him toward death, whose insistence he would fight using tools designed more for planting than uprooting. He would leave the harvest to us, those he trusted to manage his tenderness. We were his "angels," his friends, who, despite our best intentions often flitted too close to our dying friend's artificial light.

It was parable-like, his plan, more akin to how he imagined God envisioning the harvest. He would need people to do his job for him, take up what he hoped would be reconciliation on a limited basis for the few, Mary and Daniel, his sister and brother, especially. He knew his parents would never agree to such a plan without full repentance on his part and renunciation of his grievous sin. His parents preferred his destruction. They failed to recognize that in feasting on his demise they were wolfing down themselves. They would be faithful to the end, David's end, and that they had to uproot the weed that was their son.

When I think of David these days, when between sips of beer and surrounded by friends, I imagine the party with him seated nearby, holding court. He smiles and asks us to take care of his parents and encourages me to leave whatever harvest I imagined for his parents to God. In those moments, I know I have failed.

During the three years David and I knew each other, not once did I consider raising the gate of my heart to those who, by my estimation, were lying in wait to hurt and undermine my friend with their brand of religion, a religion whose shelf life was as open-ended and as frightening as the longest apocalypse. I failed to put myself in a different position, out in front, offering, proposing, or playing by a different faith rule—engaging a wrong with as much love and blessing and forgiveness as it takes to change my life for the better. It has never been my sense of how to improve my corner of the neighborhood—to look at what I perceive as evil in the eye and give back a blessing. It is not my nature to love people I cannot stand with a tender heart and humble mind. It is rare that I extend myself toward other people's pain and disappointment, especially when they are misbehaving out of it. I cannot listen to their stories, even the stories behind the stories, without a modicum of judgment. It feels right.

During our time together, I missed sacred prompts, regularly choosing my faith vocabulary without the benefit of a thesaurus. I was wrong in a way I never imagined. I participated in the giddiness of religion, that feeling of euphoria revealed in the comic state of religion when people seek, even need, ways to be offended, when the need to be right supersedes and proves more promising that any consideration of kindness. I dismissed David's parents as unworthy of sober reflection, respect, and attention. They were perpetrators of a religious experience that could hold no place in my heart.

Faith does warn when it is dying. It dies when I choose unwisely, repeatedly, when the idols to which I give my allegiance never convene because they fear my possible apostasy. Faith succumbs without putting up a fight, granting me the freedom to choose what I will spiritually reinforce and assign to my rationalizations. Righteous anger would serve as my faith idol, its tensile strength that of a communion wafer. I would learn too late that righteous anger is as limp as prophetic adverbs. It can never calm my religious insecurities or serve as the theological justifier for my deeper passions. Its beauty will eventually wilt and wither when I return to the bloom that is my life alone.

Until I met David, I had not considered the state of my faith for years. My mother handed it down to me after she received it from her mother and father. She assumed its validity and strength without references. I understand at some level the impotence of second-hand faith, but to dismiss any person's opinion just because she happens to be your parent is careless. I fell into faith, as did my brothers and sisters, although more than one of them conceded they felt pushed.

My family tree is leafed with ministers. After reading some of their sermons, I imagined the number of spirits condemned to rot on whatever battlefield they conjured from their biases. I know Abels and just as many Cains. I prefer the Abel side of the family, and yet God has given me both, that I am, if I read the psalmist correctly, *"to welcome the heritage that falls to me"* (Psalm 16:6). If, as St. Paul says, *"all things work together for good for those who love God,"* (Romans 8: 28) then in giving me a mixed inheritance, God expects me to make something of it. Forgive and love; love and forgive. I thought I had freed myself from my faith past, its ghosts and emanations, but I missed how easily I became a target of the faith champions who happened to be walking near me at any particular moment in my life.

My mother believed in a God of great love and forgiveness and also a God who was never satisfied. She did many good deeds, but she rarely seemed pleased. Faith became a process of elimination, a regurgitation of denials and negations. I first knew faith as short bursts of emotions, its life expectancy as brief as the midges just outside my Northeast Ohio home. They spring forth in the early summer, quickly irritate, and just as quickly die off. To grow, to learn adult faith, I had to outgrow, unlearn even, much of what I was taught about religion. I didn't reject the religion of my ancestors, but it did entail a sorting out period to claim what is viable. Faith is a balancing act, recognizing the blessings, even the ones that come well disguised in my great-great uncle's sermons, page after page of a false image of God with whom I would have to contend.

I found myself stuck in the most dangerous of wilderness memories—returning to points of envy when I witnessed faith alive in new friends. Since David's death, I have spent enough time alone to realize I have no clue what faith entails. Does it include simple kindness, and, if so, how does that marker distinguish believers from unbelievers who exhibit kindness daily? What is faith supposed to look like to a minister who speaks of faith rationally, but has never let it rest emotionally nearby? Is the love of God and neighbor enough to lead me to the Promised Land of my final faith imaginings? Is empathy a part of any faith circle proposed, the recognition of shared pain toward those who do not believe as I do—the indignant ones, the arrogant ones, and even those who may also presume they are wrong for the best of reasons? I confess I don't have the time and floor space for entertaining such people.

To paraphrase T.S. Eliot, perhaps the most we can hope for about faith is to be wrong about it in a new way. Does its power reside in the recognition that it cannot be pinned down or compartmentalized, that faith rubs up against not just our daily misconceptions, but any future ones as well? Faith can never look like I first imagined. Its nature is to surprise, frighten even, at the thought of being wrong about what we always assumed about faith. David and I would play this out together.

In every soul resides a brutish residue of former darkness that can never be disowned. Unless a mixture of humility and kindness tames the brute, it lurks as a potential traitor, awaiting its chance to murder the soul. The desire to wound because one has been hurt, or someone we love has been damaged, is a savory appetizer and often deliciously planned. And yet, the most well-crafted rebuttal, or the infliction of an intentional wound in retaliation, will never win the day.

I now wish for those who despised David, his lifestyle, enough grace to cover their weeping at what they missed. I am drawn to the sadness of it all and my role in perpetuating the sadness. As I look back on our time together, I should have despised what my soul considered, but didn't.

There is forever a familiar spirit hovering near my heart. I sense its presence daily. If it could speak, it would confirm what I've known about myself these many years. I remember something Virginia Woolf wrote: "I hate, I love." I cannot silence it; I don't want to silence it. I will try in these pages, however, to listen to it only when it whispers, "I love." Her counsel will prove difficult because of my residual animosity toward David's parents and their accomplices.

And so, I am left to wonder: Is it enough for me to want love to be the appropriate response? It does seem preferable to puking daily contempt toward David's enemies and myself.

Since David's death, I have replayed what little of his life I knew, rejecting him as a paragon of faith and acknowledging the seeker saint in him instead, a young man who learned to consider what faith might look like if allowed to breathe on its own. He was not a Christ-figure, which, in my estimation, is a sterile and easy interpretation, emanating not from any Christ relationship but theological malformation. If one can so easily extend the attributes of Christ, then, indeed, the Christian path is meaningless and Christianity as a religion has run out of breath. David was no faith hero, but rather, as I remember him, a grand promise of such a man hoping to make a beautiful end.

We both were excommunicated from our faith homes, he by his parents and birth church. I asked for my release when I concluded my first faith family had stopped looking for me, and when I still believed I possessed a history worth remembering. We both had waffled throughout our faith lives, blown and tossed by circumstances which always seemed consequential at the time. We were spiritual kin, though I was twenty years his senior, both open to God without incessant God-talk. David found great comfort in rituals, saints, and icons, filling his life with whatever God was for him at that moment. I worshipped different idols.

I have been rightly criticized by close friends whose love for me extends to calling me out regarding my lack of perspective regarding David and my proclivity to grant David full pardon. They gently pronounce that I was cryptically drawn to his dying, that his death prodded me to deal with the faith issues that I mismanaged for years. Somewhere in my memory, I remember an early faith teacher warning me that any review of bad Christians would be terrible for my character.

I would offer this modest defense. I was drawn to David because he learned to live faith differently, even giving me lessons in what seemed to be a lost art. Our friendship was born of spiritual need. We filled each other's emptiness; we tried not to be false with each other. Along the way, we rested in this mixed bag we called faith, where precise boundaries and dichotomies are muddled and faith is revealed as a beautiful mess.

This book is a story about the reclamation of each of us, a story of an ending with different friends and without family, except peripherally. It's a story of how one young man pushed past an idea of God, a distorted view of God, and let me come along for the ride. It's a story of how it happened, and how it played out in front of new witnesses. It is a story of hope re-imagined and a comically absurd remedy for healing.

I once asked David if I could write about our time together, our friendship, our exploration of faith.

"I guess it won't hurt. I have no say in the matter. You can do what you want. I would ask that you be real. Write about how wrong I was about God and faith; write that I learned this too late. You know me as well as anyone, the ugly and the beautiful. Let Lara write the beautiful. She feels like poetry to me. You write the ugly," he smirked.

Lara possessed an innate ability to abstain from making herself disagreeable to her friends, that when a need arose, it was not discredited by irritating associations. Her love of knowledge co-existed in her mind with the finest capacity for humility. I have never met a person having less of that fault, a principal obstacle to friendship, of reproducing the tiresome and familiar parts of one's character.

    I will write the ugly and maybe the love. David's story is a releasing of his cursed and blessed life to better friends. I hope that as his story unfolds, you will find him pleasant enough to want him as a faith friend. And me.

Chapter Three

Someone or Something Dies on Every Wilderness Journey

Pursue some path, however narrow and crooked, in which you can walk with love and reverence. Henry David Thoreau

David and I were lost together, penitent souls in search of a lashing. We violated prescribed ways of living morally and ethically, seeking love in relationships not assigned. "I loved each one for a night," David shared, insisting I never compare his deeper darkness to mine. "I even remember some of their names." We spoke of the inadequacy of confession offered to those we wounded and betrayed.

"It's not enough," I said. "It puts too much on the people I've hurt. What do they do with it, my confession? They wait for it, savor it, maybe irritated that it didn't come sooner. They are now required to reconsider how they feel about me? The confessor has an easier go. Acknowledge, admit, and move on. I walk away and leave them trying to rethink a relationship."

"Too many conditions, too many layers," David said. "I can confess my part in the ending of the relationship. I can even admit I am completely at fault. But what if I still have no desire to be reconciled to them? Confession doesn't eliminate the bitterness I once felt toward them. My relationship with them was strained for a reason. It may not be a good reason, but it's my reason. I confess because until I do, reconciliation is impossible; but confession is a step, one step."

"I know I can't force forgiveness," he continued in a way that buried all objections to his argument. "I can't expect them to forgive me immediately. Maybe they have rules, conditions to which I must abide. Maybe forgiveness is first for me. But I can't help but think I'm still leaving the heavy lifting to them."

"I think you are expecting, hoping even for something you know is not possible," I said flippantly, voicing a piece of realism into the conversation and on to David that he was not ready to hear and I was too ready to share.

"And I think you can be condescending," he countered. Back and forth, we talked, acknowledging each other, and trusting that we didn't have to mention God. We shared an ordinary strength; we were earthen vessels that contained a repository of faith expressions imparted to us through our sacred texts, our doctrines and creeds, purchased theologies, and, most significantly, our understanding of the institutional church.

They all proved to be clay pots, prone to crack and leak, crumble and break. We found ourselves at different times in our lives, and for various reasons, seeking something more, a spiritual construct we had never imagined. We were lost to regrettable faith choices—seeking the best seats in the kingdom, expecting tawdry little miracles to keep us interested in God. It can be said that we were, in Shakespeare's words, "molded out of faults," and maybe becoming a little better, even wiser, for being a little bad, theologically speaking.

And at some point in our relationship, we embraced "lostness" as a possible starting point, a first dip into a different theological pool, floating the idea of God as sacred mystery. Our rules of faith changed.

Lostness is not darkness, emptiness, or hopelessness, although these are the peripheral friends of Job. They have something to teach. Their depths must be mined, but lostness is not nothingness. It is not intellectual laziness or spiritual bypassing—the avoidance of confronting uncomfortable feelings, unresolved wounds, and damning sins. It is not a willing indifference to life. And it is not theological fascism.

Lostness is a path of uncertainty, especially as it relates to God and faith and sacred texts. It is a hopeful revealing that as one travels unsure, without maps, one brushes up against the holy in different ways. David and I envisioned a new spiritual home. We packed sparingly, releasing burdensome faith positions and theological toiletries before setting out on our uncertain and surprising adventure.

"Lostness" holds significant power if one is willing to pause long enough to tap into its possibilities. It does not release such energy without proper accreditation, however. It is surprisingly flirty and quickly put off. It forever tempts a return to certainty. It's strength, ironically, wanes when one is most vulnerable and considering returning to the prison of absolute belief.

To consider "lostness" as a spiritual path also requires a death notice—one's own or someone else's. Death, as the natural ending of life, its cessation and some notification, and death, metaphorically, to a manufactured idea of God or one's remedial understanding of the God of one's own making.

Death, and its summons, is often violent and unexpected and threatening. It also orders the "proper self," as Shakespeare notes, to open oneself to a profound strength. To consider faith differently, to think of God beyond the strictures once taught and absorbed over the years, insists we dive face-first into the number of days we have left.

I watched David die, finally. I knew him only as a dead man walking in thrift store Birkenstocks, pardoned so often the executioner regularly called in sick, saying, "Why bother?" When we prayed, which was sporadic and often perfunctory, David mentioned a "good death," which certainly included the cessation of his physical pain, but also for the healing of his feelings of bitterness and anger and resentment toward those who wished his suffering.

"I just assumed I would die old, maybe in my sleep after a half-way decent life. But how old is old. And won't we always miss out on something? I get so much time. What will I do with what is available to me?"

"Is it a good life?" I asked. "Let me answer for you. I know it is. It will be too short, but it's a decent life."

"You make it sound like I get an reward," he said.

David died on a Thursday evening, sometime near nine, his ending imperceptible—a soft, choppy, inhalation, and then nothing. No final expiration. No last warning that this was the end of our journey together. Nothing. He was alive and now dead. His soul vanished in a puff to some distance, a wisp of smoke lifting from aromatic cedars burning in a dark wood. I was alone now, left behind, unsure of much of anything. I found some comfort believing David was now better informed.

He slipped from me, and I didn't reach for him, as per his instructions. I watched his body—post-hole thin, splotchy, his blood pooling near the surface of his skin like a new oil find. Blistered and bruised, his body barely registered an indention on what I perceived as uncomfortable sheets. His elbows looked for skin; his joints still arthritic embers, even as his body grew cold. I cringed when the nurses repositioned his body for the first post-mortem inspection.

David was dead. I witnessed his last sigh, what I knew was his most defiant sigh, his final fuck you to his pain—so constant, unrelenting, and debilitating, teasing him the last three years with relief in fitful pauses. And then there was his physical pain now managed in his death.

The hospital room was stark, icebox cold, an appropriate sterile receptacle for new corpses. His bed, the centerpiece, and one hideous chair, positioned in the corner next to a tray, broke up the spartan ambiance of some misguided minimalist decorator on retainer. The room looked like what I imagined when I let myself imagine David dead.

A nurse peeked into the room and nodded, offering the kind of smile caregivers smile, a gentle upturn of the corner of her lips. It was a simple gesture, a prayer even. She returned later to bathe him, after the appropriate time, the "kairos" time, as the Greeks are want to suggest, the time for my first regrets, if onlys. She washed his body as if he was about to receive company.

I sat numb, averting my eyes from his corpse. When I returned to his face, drawn and flat and gray, I glimpsed peace. I let myself imagine this man, fully incarnated in time, brimming now with enthusiasm, the mystery of God revealed, the God in whom he had become thoroughly invested.

"I wrote about mother," he shared a week before his death. "Had to face something that has been messing with my mind. It kept seeping into my heart. I don't like it. I thought I managed it earlier. I get so tired of feelings that don't stay dead. You beat them down, but they are a weed. They keep showing up. Even after I am dead, mother can't afford remorse, at least not publicly. I can't get my head around her disconnect from me, and what side rails she needs to keep her feelings in the correct lane. My dying is not going to be some elixir. She can't drink her sorrow. She just can't."

I watched his resurrected body. At what point did God come and wave his spirit home? He knew resurrection, to which I became a witness. Cruelly, before his resurrection, he experienced a crucifixion at the hands of family, his early church, some of whom fulfilled the Judas role by betraying the new model of love David offered them.

David was the oldest child of Peter and Nora Pryn. While on its surface, that sentence appears harmless enough, revealing little more than birth order. It would play out as one of the most emotionally harsh sentences I've ever written. As the oldest, David would be the first to fall, toppled by religious slogans culled from his mother Nora's family Bible. If theology is rudimentary God-talk, David's parents needed to read more before speaking. They expected too much from talking, puking up their emotional bile, enough for a lifetime of pain administered to spiritual addicts. They equated silence with weakness. They lived ready-made answers, even though they appeared theologically illiterate.

God resembled their moral purposes—severe and unrelenting. They worshipped the god of the half-grin, more smirk than smile, the god of the darkest and bloodiest hymn. Into this home, David was born to shackled believers, imprisoned voluntarily, parents who found bewildering comfort in never having to consider the strength of the bars of their spiritual cell. They read the Bible through the lens of an endless summer of "monkey trials." For the best of intentions and the worst of reasons, they battled against a different truth to defend their tenuous beliefs, forgetting that God does not have to be protected. Faith was a mere caricature and God looked like what they knew first.

There are times when we are captive to the tragedies of our first faith traditions. They are so familiar, almost natural to us. They exclude the possibility that the same feelings and ideas might be expressed differently through someone else's faith tradition. To entertain the hope that we might find our spiritual selves in the literature, rites, and symbols of others is a gift, even though at first the gifts may seem distorted and alien to us. New spiritual truths that transcend time and space and death are born in metaphorical vessels. Engaging God only in a world of doctrine, or through hard unidimensional facts handed down to future generations without commentary or reflection, is to miss much.

The Pryns were angry "faithers," insistence their daily toddy. They were people who managed daily disappointment with God and accused their loved ones instead. They dressed as spiritual pirates, looting their children's spirit, and David was first in line, the first victim. They plundered, taking what was precious about faith—its mystery and incompleteness—and left behind baubles, the faith trinkets from their religious carnival, worthless in value on any promising market.

"My parents have always been more believers than parents," David shared. "They are 'deep breath' people. At first, you are forced to inhale what they are spouting. Then you find the strength to exhale and realize they are never going to be what you wish they would be for you. I'm not sure when it happened, but I had to learn to endure my parents."

On multiple occasions, David shared how he could live in the same house, be forced to leave, and why he returned to Seneca.

"I'm dying," he said. "I came to Seneca to be near them. I know that doesn't make sense, crazy even, but I have no money. I get a disability check and a Medicaid card. Dad slips me money each month. My mother doesn't know. You'd be surprised at how much hypocrisy you can muster when you are dying. "

Weaned on spiritual smugness, the Pryns transitioned to harshness effortlessly and without reflection. They could quickly name the depth and intensity of others' depravity.

"You don't get to name the ways you are lost with Mother, even Dad, but more mother. You would think they would be tired," David shared, "having had to beat back unconditional love for generations."

While never extensive, their reach was long enough to wound with regularity—family mostly, some friends specifically, and always David, their oldest. Their faith perspective was absolute, hardened, and shaped by years of listening to the same voices singing the same song. It protected them like a shield and freed them from any scintilla of doubt that their son might stumble upon a different faith party.

Surprisingly, David learned to like God again late, when it mattered, when his life, spent and most frail, found release from his parents' threats. Over a period of ten years, he excised from his spirit their history of indoctrination.

"I think I was in my late twenties, maybe earlier, I can't remember exactly, but I couldn't feel God. I begged God for something, anything. And then it hit me. I would never find God until I let my parents go. I didn't want them out of my life, but emotionally I couldn't find God with them hanging around waiting to come down on me. I had fumbled with the lid of my pot of faith for years, seeking some way to believe in a God I could get along with, live with, without sacrificing everything about me. I made the decision to break that jar. I smashed it in anger and cried myself to sleep."

"So, you ran from God for your own protection and safety?' I asked, exhibiting what David reminded me was my most annoying habit—thinking I was an active listener.

"God turned out not to be the problem. It was Mom and Dad. For most of my life they won. I don't remember thinking about anything consciously, learning to see God with more sophistication, but in that moment, I knew it was important not to give them an inch. I had to stop caring if mother was comfortable. I didn't wake up on Wednesday determined to prove my parents wrong. I just started with an idea. God could look different from my mother. And I decided to risk my soul's consignment to hell for eternity. What was I really risking? The God of terrible judgment felt like hell already."

He ceded his early faith to bitter descendants, his parents mostly, but also their supporters—the "tiresome herd," David's name for them—the people present to his parents, playing multiple roles of assurance for them. Their job? Reinforce for his parents, as well as the fragile and the wounded and the unsure, that words like grace, mercy, and forgiveness were bought and paid for by their particular brand of repentance. David was dying when I met him. He had already been named as dead by the "herd." Their role was to protect their brand, insisting the Pryns beat back any feeling of sustained empathy toward their son, those fleeting moments when one considers the possibility one might be wrong. The Pryns' compassion for their son was always more whisper than shout and never flowed with enough force to cover their profound grief over David's choices and his sexual orientation.

The god they named, the god of the club, their club, was fashioned with golden restrictions—a hand-me-down god, an idol, a god who promised comfort and assurance as long as they lived out the god prescriptions. David served as a test case for their methodology—how they understood God and what God expected of them. What would they do with this young man who was the perfect foil? His was no nebulous sin, resisting any delicate name, the sin behind closeted doors. This foil had a face, and parents, a mother and father who spent too many mournful days praying to God to return their son to them in a more acceptable form.

There is an inadequacy in "foundness" if it must play out in a prescribed way. To be found is often the culmination of multiple lost points surrounding lost people. And the temptation is to manipulate some happy ending. One day, I wish I remembered it as a Monday, but it felt like a Monday, one of those days you want to give away, David began recalibrating defensive postures. I remember it as a day of low spirits for David. The lesions on his brain were increasing in intensity and frequency, causing severe headaches. He surprised me between gulps of water and choking down narcotics.

"If AIDS is supposed to be this wake-up call, if it is supposed to pull or push me toward reconciliation with my family and with God, I don't want it. I'm not sure I can agree to the terms. I don't want to be restored to people who forced me out, who don't even like me. And, pastor, you need to know I've never bought into the death-bed confession or reconciliation. Who benefits from that? It won't be me. I guess I can be dead on their terms, however. Listen, pastor, I'm up for forgiveness; I can acknowledge my regrets, my part in the destruction, but I will not give up my birthright. I'm a child of God fashioned out of the clay of homosexual soil. He paused, holding his glass with both hands while inching his shoulders against his pillows. "And there's always a catch in being 'found'. It doesn't feel true."

There is an inability of "foundness" to satisfy completely. It's the brief ease of spirit one feels in the first minutes of a family reunion when a physical face can, for a moment, beat back what one has always known as an ugly soul. David found strength, not in the idea of being found, but in remembering when he lost the grasp of his soul and why he had to fight daily against the temptation to be drawn back to those who happily judged the darker elements of his life. Why would he ever consider returning to them? He felt emboldened, as certain as any seeker, and found whatever strength he needed to protect what he now had clearly defined as most dear. His faith principles, compromised because he had no place to lay his head, saved him. He resigned himself to his secondary hypocrisy. He would take his father's money when offered and would be grateful. "What's a little hypocrisy if it serves a greater end?" he shared. He could live physically near his parents but never emotionally near them. He planted hedges to protect his soul. His parents would walk a parallel path near him but still close enough to be heard.

David died isolated and ostracized from his family. He refused to relinquish his heart to their darker world. Pushing forward with a different understanding of faith meant estrangement. How does one walk with those whose hands are in their pocket, who can retrieve in an instant both dagger or flower without prompting? Estrangement, its echo reverberating in his fragile spirit, had to be acknowledged, then eliminated, no matter the volume. He had to let his parents go.

David had lived too long with the deadly consequences of banking his life on what he had once received, or had withheld, by those he had chosen to love early. He released them, those who had failed to be gentle with his soul and who failed to beat back for him what he could only destroy.

Any spiritual journey is undertaken alone. By its nature, it is solitary. Expecting bishops and rabbis and ministers to make it for us is to miss the possibilities. The inertia of organized religion is a constant challenge to spiritual growth. Inevitably, we must make our path rather than follow someone else's. We enter the woods at its darkest point where no one has cut a path before. Even as we fall, we discover the beauty of flora and fauna.

Chapter Four

Moving Forward Incrementally

Some rise by sins and some by virtue fall. Some condemned for a fault alone. Shakespeare, Measure for Measure.

I liked David, not because he had an unhappy time of it. No, I liked him because he learned to move his horizon forward, incrementally, fighting the tug of his past, and finally resting in his most precious consolation—he would determine the pace of his final walk.

Some protested that it was too much to ask a seventeen-year-old to defy his family, early culture, and his heavy-handed spiritual heritage in order to pursue a different spiritual dream. I would agree. The price of such self-realization is never cheap, at times unthinkable given the obstacles placed in David's path. Still, he chose at the end of his life to pursue the marvelous and consider the unthinkable.

There was a celebration in his head which agitation and anxiety were throwing. Crashing the party was a new consideration for him, that his life could be rearranged. He was a son, brother, friend, enemy, sexual malcontent, seeker, and doubter. Along the way, he claimed a new identity, that as a child of God he could be many more things, maybe anything.

"I think I have always been happy to be alive, gay or not, even as I struggled," he said. "I have this idea of God buried in my head. I've stopped digging for anything more. I find comfort in the idea of God now more than ever."

He learned to lift his sights which, he explained, first involved the "great forgetting," but, when pressed, he said, was not "forgetting" at all.

"It's more compartmentalization with an attitude shift…my attitude. I have to do all the moving. It's the first lesson, really, the most important lesson, knowing what I can and cannot expect from those who knew me first," he shared.

He excited himself in possibility. As damned as he was by others' estimation, he chose to no longer live only in regrets. There were moments, as brief as a grace glimpse, when he made damnation seem attractive. He was hardly the first person who rejected the gods of false prophets, people who sipped on doubt as easily and gleefully as one would chug an afternoon beer. He was a believer, was always a believer, but he refused to grovel because he was dying. or even repent in order for his parents to feel comfortable signing off.

I found David restless in bed most days. He shifted his skeleton frame in his bed, its contours and indentions and folds punishing each movement. Finding little relief, he often suggested we move outside to the steps leading to his apartment. "I need to smoke." There we rested, inhaling a fragile silence present before most awkward conversations.

"My mother feels that the one who is lost in a family, by being lost, is the one who has to move. That means reconciliation will always begin with me. I don't like her definition. I am the villain; I should know and feel the wound. That's what she said in her letter, that I'm the reason for Dad's heart problems, and that I need to ask for forgiveness. It's just another layer. I'm lost to her because I'm gay. She really has no idea how great is my lostness. I've used people, pastor, repeatedly—a lot of people. Don't ask for testimonials at my memorial service," he said, drawing so deep on his cigarette his cheeks cratered.

"It won't be pretty. I can give you details if you are up to it," he continued. I smiled. I loved details, the bits and pieces of a person's story. I loved the gossip, but wanted more. I wanted to know more about his mother, a woman who appeared to have done a great deal of good in her life, but rarely welcomed. For much of my life, I wanted to devise a way to accommodate the Pryn's tragedy by asking what was missing from their stories. I can't help but wonder about their terrible foregrounding in which their souls withered and died. Surely, their "sickness unto death" preceded their consignment of their son to their idea of hell. They could not, would not, present themselves to us as ambassadors of life. And what I have to say about them has little to do with any currently fashionable grace accounts of them from strangers. Rumor and hearsay cannot sustain for any length of time. I invited their participation and perspective in the writing of this book. They refused. And I confess the pleasures of possession by memory of them. They have sustained me for more than a decade. There are times, however, I think I wish it were not so. The natural progression of any hoped-for intimacy, playing out in moments I never considered significant, proved impossible. We consigned ourselves to finding the best seats to witness David's death.

"I've ignored so many of life's good markers, simple decency is one of them," he shared. "My mother believes I'm lost. She's right, but she only knows a little. She doesn't have a clue as to how lost I was. There is a part of me, the shitty side, that would enjoy filling in all the details for her. You know, just to see her face. Maybe I'll read my journal to her for some night-time reading," he said. "She can name my lostness. I won't take that from her. She needs it for the divide between us to continue. But I've lived pastor; I know the raw material."

David stopped short. He did not expand further, which I learned to accept grudgingly. He grew tired. "I think I'll try and nap again...fitful sleep, naps really, but I get some relief, and one more day toward my dying can be crossed off. I have only a number of days left."

I enrolled in David's life late, sparingly present at first to the softer consequences of his dying. I misread his life early, having packed his physical outline with inchoate ideas about him, building up for my purposes a whole crowd of details of his life as a dying gay man.

I stormed onto David's desperate stage, positioning myself in his struggle, uninvited, leaning into his vulnerability, seeking merely, at first, rumor's substantiation—his alienation from his family as he made preparations to close his life. I didn't know it at the time, but I would be a witness to his emotional execution.

I served as David's minister by default. Our church was located one block from his apartment, on the corner of Main and Maple Streets. I had little to offer him other than a job description. I dithered on the cusp of compassion because it was expected of me. I filled my room with my own personality until I thought no more of the room than of myself. I did what grown men do when face to face with suffering and unfairness. I preferred not to see it.

David managed me tenderly, positioning me around his life, and fashioning enough emotional space for both of us. He emptied himself willingly to me, still clinging to his nobility and melancholy, and content to reside in such transubstantiation. He invited our church and me to his pathetic homecoming. We enrolled in his life with no real thought of what we might learn. We began timidly, warily, following only what we hoped was compassion's path.

To David's family, we were not only misinformed, we were also careless, fabricating a context that didn't exist. What his family would never understand was we were classically offended. We had formed ideas about them, ideas that would forever hold a principal place, regardless of additional revelatory truth presented to us as a defense.

"My mother despises me," David shared one peaceful evening in April.

"And your father?" I asked.

"Dad? Well, he pities me, pities that his son is sick. I know where I stand with mother; I have no illusions. When you think about it, pity is such a weak emotion, second cousin to 'I'm praying for you.' Pity is basically 'I'm glad I'm not you.' I don't need pity, and I don't have time to drag someone toward compassion. Pastor, don't let your prayers for me be about pity. If I could, I would insist on approving all prayers on my behalf. But since I can't, just let compassion win out. It's a big enough emotion for all the shit I'm dealing with."

Any definition of "lostness," beyond the construction presented by religionists, beyond bending to the sway of negation, inevitably includes mapping our lives according to the number of heart slights revealed and absorbed into our spirits. They are the twinges, real or imagined, when we give our lives and hearts to that which is minor, our spirits to that which is less, and our lives to those who do not deserve such a prominent place. It is the day we wake and realize we are more than we imagined in God's eyes.

How easily we concretize our lives according to these heart slights, pushing past any number of markers that offer a different review of our lives, those gentle reminders of the danger of becoming "less than." So often, generational markers, set forth by our personal company of saints, dead or alive, carry the day. Poorly, yes, but they carry the day.

Is there a point in time, as we shuffle toward death, that forces some reexamination, some acknowledgment, that we possess the raw material to live out our faith confident in our "lostness?" The strength of lostness is never worrying about who wins the memorial service. We do what we can and give our souls to better friends who write well and will speak effectively on our behalf.

David slowly began to name for me the steps of his soul's development: The multiple recalibrations of what he had been force-fed and what he would have to accede to, at least on the surface, in Seneca because he needed a bed. It was remarkable, this shift, prompted by some idea that cannot be explained or taken in emotionally unless one is a witness to it. He was dying, and he had so little time to do what he needed to do.

He gave minimal emotional energy to the time he had left, although he knew it would be soon. David's doctors probed around the periphery, using jargon that revealed their discomfort in anything final. His body didn't care anymore. He did want to die at thirty-three.

"Jesus died at thirty three, he said."

He spent little time thinking about a future destination or afterlife, preferring his present hell's breathable air instead. "If God is good, God will take care of all the practical stuff," he shared. He would repurpose his soul, recognizing his soul's innate power to both maim and heal, that his soul would expand or wither by the direction he chose to travel.

"I didn't sleep," he mumbled as I came into the bedroom one afternoon, sidestepping the folded laundry encircling his bed. "Step over Camille's mess. That woman keeps me in clean clothes."

"The pain pills didn't help, huh?" I asked.

"Oh, they worked. I just didn't want to sleep. When you are dying, waking up is distressingly important. I was thinking some awful things last night. It wasn't a good night for God. I blamed God for a while. Not that I have AIDS, but it sure seems like the consequences are too severe. It's my new go-to emotion."

We spoke about prayer on multiple occasions. David believed in prayer, its power or lack thereof. He insisted that God answered his prayers, and that his conversations with God each night could be and should be as easy as speaking to a close friend. He and God spent hours together, mostly at night, when the light from the streetlamp outside his window nibbled away at the darkness trying to envelop his room. His ritual—pulling the blanket over his eyes, playing hide and seek with the night, imagining where it and God would first touch his body.

By most scholarly opinions, his understanding of prayer would be considered simplistic, something one would learn in Sunday School—God as a furry friend. But there was something profoundly blessed in his method, not in the way he addressed God, but what they talked about. He did not ask for the most pressing of miracles, his physical healing. He had resigned himself to the fact that he was going to die and soon. If God chose to heal him, he would be just as surprised as his mother, whose understanding of prayer was protection from sin and that her son was reaping the consequences of his sin.

David viewed prayer differently: He wanted someone to witness to a different part, a better part, of his life. God would do.

"People hear some crazy shit while praying, don't they pastor?"

"A lot of bad praying out there," I countered as if I had a clue about prayer.

"They say its God," he continued. "I guess I'm no different. I do take some comfort that my idea of God isn't violent or out to get me. Pastor, did you know I sometimes swear in my prayers. It's part of me. You have to be honest, right pastor? When I pray, I try not to make my case. I believe God is good and love and looking for me. That's enough for me. I've been wrong about God most of my life. Maybe I'm wrong now. I'll know soon enough. But my prayers feel like they are mine, just mine. I can try and blame God, mother and dad, for screwing up my faith, but it's really on me. I know I didn't want their faith, but for too long I've been lazy about finding my own."

"Pastor," he said, a designation I would learn to accept, having been named his confessor and given the sacred task of listening to his life, "being wrong about faith doesn't have to be a bad thing, does it, a deal-breaker with God? I'm right about that, yes."

"I know a lot of people who build their faith on another person's work," I answered.

"I get that, now, but I always thought of faith as assurance, certainty, a way to walk instead of a trip to take. That's all I ever knew. There is something defeating about knowing that now. What would have happened to me if, as a gay man, I knew God only wanted to walk with me? Maybe that's why I like the Holy Spirit more than Jesus. Jesus has a place in my heart, but that's a problem—he has a place. And the Holy Spirit blows where it will. It never has a home. And I want to feel the breeze."

David first found some wisp of unconditional love, consequences be damned, in the emotional safety net of the gay community in Columbus. Hell, he shared, and described in frightening detail by his childhood pastor, was a place of eternal torment for the unrepentant, a gated community for his kind. It was preferable to David than any prospect of future paradise whose only entrance requirement was a closeted identity.

In Columbus, he grew strong enough to name his ground, insisting that whatever mud on his everyday shoes be acknowledged, affirmed even, even if he had been walking in shit. He became acutely aware that trespassing on his ground were villains of all sorts and kinds—notable conspirators using him to fashion a reason for their judgment.

"I don't have much time for bullshit. It took me some time to name my particular bullshitters, but I did it. I named them all," he shared, sitting at his scratched table, initials of people he didn't know carved in the legs, people as unknown to him as his parents. His multiple Mother Mary icons looked mercenary in his subsidized apartment, keeping watch over him and his pornographic postcard which served as a bookmark for his five-volume portable library.

"My parents let me go," he said. "No. That's not right. They cast me away after reparative therapy failed to produce the desired results. It's a brutal thing when religion makes parents choose, but you'd think choosing your child would always win out."

Chapter Five

The Danger of Shrines

> *... Someone I loved once gave me a box full of darkness.*
> *It took me years to understand that this, too, was a gift.* Mary Oliver, **Thirst**

I wish I could be a true believer. It's an attractive proposition, so my first faith friends remind me on those all too frequent times these days when we brush up against each other around our parents' ashes and framed pictures. We manage our suspicions with each other as gently as possible and without significant pretense. When I walked away from my faith home, I left behind some scrap of my heart and my care for these friends who loved me despite my perpetual hypocrisy. They wished more for me, even creating allowances for me, giving me enough space to decide if this faith thing had any staying power in my life, if it would win the day, finally.

I loved them for their concern first presented to me fifty years ago; I love them now, despite their superior grins, for the memories that warm me to this day and the freedom they granted me to be as much of an agnostic as I needed to be as I made my way. When I think of them, usually just after twilight, when darkness has yet to consume the sunset, I feel sad. Despite all that I've experienced these forty years since we've listened to each other, I want them to answer for me the one question that never leaves my spirit: Do they know there are other voices than the sure, the certain?

Faith as propositional assent and pledging absolute loyalty to a set of theological principles works for them. They fear for my soul because true-believing no longer works for me.

They consider me now on the edge of Christianity, teetering next to oblivion, because of my jettison of long-time convictions about what should give my life meaning but no longer serves me well.

I am not stridently averse to believing their way. It would undoubtedly make my faith journey easier. Still, there is the history of true-believing I must avoid or ignore: The church's violent history to marginalize and its inquisition of spiritual pain inflicted on non-believers to compartmentalize. The dues required of true belief seem prohibitive. How much will certainty cost me? Am I paying too much, all while consigning my soul to a lesser god? What is the price I am willing to pay for letting go of that which will be easier to acquire for something more demanding? Faith wisdom is at least discerning that the thing gained is better than the thing being taken away or let go.

True believing is a fitful place to reside for any length of time if one is given to exhilaration. I confess trying to be a true believer has not been worth the effort. Still, I am forever mystified by true belief's charm; faith as a promise, an assurance, that at some future point, I will be found in the heaven of my own making.

My first faith invitation was in pamphlet form, my rules for the faith dance, which I assumed was tucked strategically inside my crib by my mother. My early faith friends received the same invitation, but we interpreted it differently. The invitation assumed far too much and required far too little of me, except an acknowledgment of God, which I have never considered a problem. But getting to God beyond simple assent required I see the ellipsis and what was missing from my faith walk. My teachers promised my confession of belief, the verbal and very public acknowledgment of my soul's sinful state, would serve as my protection against whatever evil I might encounter on my faith path. They were sincere but misinformed. The faith foundation they promised turned out to be the best rates on shifting sand.

I would have to find a way to believe that was my own. The burden of too many seasons of inattention and sloppiness, too much time, days and nights reading and writing about other's faith and wishing it my own no longer worked. I could no longer pilfer the nuggets of faith expressed by my friends without the necessary theological investment by me.

I possessed no particular theological skills. I thought only about trying understand God differently, but I was told scripture allowed only so much excavation. I did like the idea of a faith that encouraged a different interpretation, one that removed God as a cosmic bellhop; maybe one that allowed enough leeway, even carelessness, while navigating specific texts. It would take years but I would learn to eliminate my need for loopholes while reading my stories of faith, one that rejected foisting mindless answers on the suffering and leaving them alone, grief-stricken, and letting God move as quickly or slowly as God felt was needed.

To exercise the rules of scripture's faith dance, presented as infalliable, was to miss much. As far as I could see, its Price is Right prize is the gift to utilize partial evidence and hearsay to win the moment, to earn the right to be right to define faith definitively for all who unfortunately orbited my life. Along the way, someone was always diminished, judged openly, and with minimal reflection. These days, the hungry child with a name in Darfur becomes just another hungry child to support with relief. To consider faith is to see the bodies of all hungry children as our own, the pain of humanity as our own. Until then, faith is a word, a throwaway word, a selfish word, deserving of every ridicule. Faith, assigned as rules, tempted me to spend too much time looking for loopholes or avoiding inconsistencies, those places in my sacred text that benefiedt me as I sought some faith advantage.

I can never be a true believer because of the Bible, not because of the stories or their misuse by people of faith over the centuries, but because of how God is presented in the stories: Eden's bliss fucked up by fresh fruit and freewill, and original blessing thwarted by God and later promulgated by St. Augustine's repressive understanding of sexuality; the Hebrews wandering for forty years and punished by God for having the audacity to consider the devil they knew and wanting to return to their old slavery in Egypt. When the remnant finally arrived at their Promised Land, Jericho would have to be annilhilated, all the women, men, children, and animals because of what they heard as God's malevolent instructions.

In Genesis, I read about the Tower of Babel, humanity's first dust-up with idolatry. Their attempt to reach beyond the layers of heaven to find God failed miserably, but it was their idolatry, their first whisper of defiance. Despite their muddled presuppositions, the people formulated a religious system that would forever serve as the scaffolding for later generation's multiple towers that, for some, make God unnecessary.

The Tower revealed the first faith sounds of my ancestors. The repetitive thuds of claw hammers and trowels called my ancestors to the God they mistakenly assumed they wanted, the God hidden just beyond the natal star, and just beyond their best efforts and reach. At some point God muted their attempt at independence, or so say the scribes who intepreted God as insecure and who needed protection from whatever threat the writers imagined God to take seriously. I can't help but wonder if the people had built a two-story split level instead of a skyscraper, would they have been allowed?

What was I to do with God asking Abraham to sacrifice Isaac, his only son, as a test to see if Abraham's faith was genuine? Who can make sense of a God who would ask a parent to do such a thing? I let myself consider how dangerous is this God of ours. What is there about the story that we do not know? Where was Isaac's mother, Sarah, in this treason? Would she have not at least run interference if she knew of such a diabolical plan? And Isaac, the little one, would he ever be the same? Would he ever be able to trust his father and his father's God again?

Similarly, there is the story of Jephthah's careless and blasphemous vow to God, his willingness to offer his daughter as a sacrifice if God would grant his first wish upon his Disney Star. It cannot be defended. His frivolous understanding of prayer, his careless speaking God's name, and his obstinate obsession to follow through without a do-over is blasphemy. I can't believe in this God of evil distortions.

And little Samuel would grow up with Eli for God's sake, whose parenting style can only be described as indifferent, Phinneas and Hophni the collateral damage. Samuel, who would eventually trade a faith first expressed in humility, in belief that offered no clear direction, whose sole prerequisite was a willing heart, for a God made in his image—nationalistic, vengeful beyond even the most sordid contemplation, and bloodthirsty. He grew into a faith bully.

While not as theologically troubling as many stories, there is the comedy routine of a talking, God-fearing, donkey who sees better than his master Balaam, a self-proclaimed prophet and seer. How can someone be both sharp-eyed and lacking in clarity of vision at the same time?

These stories, these problematic stories are the fodder by which I first examined my faith, troubled the water, and asked me to play a role, even as a minor character. Each one required I refrain from peeking behind the curtain. The untruths about God, perpetuated by well-meaning adults, were eventually exposed as I began to make my first step toward faith. I made a choice: Do I continue the numbing and stuffing down, or begin the deep soul work that this new season of life demanded I finally face. These stories, and countless others, are the same stories by which those who have little regard for God, or any respect for God, refer to in their tiresome attempts to promote atheism at parties where politeness at avoiding controversial topics like religion are violated with regularity.

On the surface, the stories appear tame enough, but upon further reflection, reveal that the God of the Hebrew scriptures was a problem. Initially, I tried to make excuses for God, my first soiree at learning to be an interpreter, a much-too-young interpreter for sure, but an interpreter nonetheless. I sensed I needed other tools, but I was not privy to these tools. I would have to manufacture some method of interpretation built from whatever was left of my first faith and its charming inconsistencies.

Unexpectedly, I experienced some peace when I begin to question the infallibility of my sacred text. Much of the world's violence can be traced to those who, at least in my tradition, mismanaged our sacred story. Scripture, while never asking for a literal reading, serves as the core of many Christians' faith. It easily becomes the deification of the Bible. I learned to worship at a different altar, dressed in my Sunday best, and carrying my best offering, my mind.

"The Southern Baptist Convention has a statement of faith where the first point is the Bible, before any mention of God," I stated during one session on learning to read the Bible again. "Talk to me."

"Text mania doesn't consider that the Bible can clarify earlier statements, arbitrate disagreements, or deal with new developments," said Joseph Beckwith, my favorite spiritual nuisance who dismissed any truce with people who regarded the authority of scripture and its easy suppositions as infallible. "But for those who need certainty," he continued, "they have to find it in the texts, and you can find anything in the texts. They have the facts, end of story. They conveniently leave wiggle room for charging exorbitant interest or excluding the foreigner, however. They are miners seeking nuggets that support their biases and beliefs; they twist phrases to prove they are honoring the Bible's words. Cafeteria Christians picking and choosing which verses to follow and with less care than they exercise in selecting a side order at Bob Evans."

David piped up, his hands trembling from the side effects of medicine, drugs timed for late morning and prescribed to let him die slowly. "Before there were any texts, there was first a story. Someone heard a story, thought it was interesting enough to write it down in mud, but it was first a story. Someone would prove to be the hero or villain, depending on how they viewed God, their culture. Someone got to decide, right? It wasn't God; it was a human being. I'm just saying I would have included different stories."

The biblical story is not just a story. It is a potent symbol of something grander and beautiful, revealing a God I never really knew. These days, when I think about the interpretive practices foisted on the Bible, I sense there are strong misreadings and weak misreadings. I also wonder if a correct reading is possible if the story does not take me to the sublime of new faith places accompanied by the surprising God. A literal reading parrots the words. It requires little effort.

The more powerful the story, the more it relies on the strength of metaphor to prod me toward a different direction. It confronts me with a word that should always be beyond my reach. As Nietzche suggests, "anything we can express is already dead in our hearts." Any consideration of the beautiful, the unimaginable, demands some measure of subjectivity and is always beyond the limited scope of ideology. I now possess a literary love for the Bible tempered by one defense which, for me, can only be the overwhelming presence of love.

As a youth, I was handed a piece of communion bread, crumbs really, without being told how the bread might nourish my soul beyond literalism. The stories were substantial enough at first to draw my beginning faith mind away from whatever dank woods housed my first real faith problem—original sin. I still felt empty, however.

I am a reluctant believer because of the one I follow who made an appearance on this planet, and because a few wise scribes reasoned someone might want to write down something of his visit. John Killinger said, "Jesus was God's answer to a bad reputation." I like that. I have a love/hate relationship with Jesus because of what he asks of me. Oh, this relentless Nazarene. He saved me from the awful habit I have of trying to save myself, of sparing my energies. He saved me for life, for the spendthriftiness of love. And his message, found in the Sermon on the Mount, contains the most hopeful conjunction ever—"but." "You have heard it said, but I say to you." This Jesus left room for me and my budding faith, a faith beyond the dance rules promulgated by people who, in my estimation, had not practiced enough to earn a judge's rating.

So, to my friends who loved me first, I offer this word: I would be lost in the dark without the light that Christianity sheds on my life, the light I find in truths like incarnation, grace, sacrament, forgiveness, blessing, and the paradoxical dance of death and regeneration. And yet, my relationship with Christianity has changed. Using Christian language is problematic for me because it has been taken hostage by theological terrorists and tortured beyond recognition.

I maintain an uneasy comfort with God, which may be profitable for both of us when we tire of each other. The traces of God I see repeatedly keep me believing today. I get this day, not tomorrow, which is just the right amount of time for the faith I can muster. Each day I awaken and breathe this simple prayer: "Can I believe again today?" If it can be said that all human beings will sacrifice their lives, their children's lives, to something—power and wealth and status—then I choose, despite my fluttering belief, to give my life to something else, someone else. Not the Jesus of John 3:16 signs blasphemed in whitewash on hillsides or on stencil on poster boards at sporting events. I see such signs and suppress screams. "Please, by all that is holy, let Jesus rest! Stop and consider who he was and is and consider this humble acknowledgment: He would never show up to most church socials."

I spend most days believing and forgetting. When I am at my weakest, I wonder, "Is it worth it," this sacrifice whose impact feels as faint as the first drop of rain that sneaks in early from an approaching thundercloud. What if, at the end, when the number of days I have left are spent, I discover, after my entry into nothingness, I was wrong? What if in some way I learn there is no reward for loving, for self-sacrifice, and genuine care for my corner of humanity? If at this time, when the echo of millions of voices mock me as the last cells of my body die away, "You have spent your life on the wrong thing," I hope to be okay, resting in whatever nothingness smells like, whatever nothingness is reserved for me, and to be content that it was worth it because of the choice I made to give myself to what I thought was something higher. I hope to look back without regret and realize my body will at least sustain the earth for other promising possibilities. That and the fact that our four score and ten in God's grand scheme is not that long to be wrong.

It's dicey, this believing thing, never mind the determiner "true" believing. It has required I take up residence in a different frame house of faith. I can't be a true believer, even though the temptation to return will be ever present when I require a dose of certainty. But for now, my membership card in the "true-believing" community has been terminated…at my request.

Letting Go of True Belief

If I know anything of the world--with all its daily horror on full display, its full-frontal inhumanity, its naked blasphemy scrolling across the screen as breaking news—it's never easy this believing thing. I don't have to keep score to know that violence and brutality are winning.

This faith thing just hasn't turned out as I thought. I haven't been disappointed necessarily because I was never sure what to expect. I had relied first on those who pretended assurance to tell me. They were the storytellers of my early faith, (which, ironically, was my mother's definition of a liar) sharing the markers I must consider on my path to becoming a true believer. What they didn't do was protect God for me, or provide God with enough cover. I won't say I was sold a bill of goods, but I learned at church camp, of all places, that my beginning faith would never carry the day.

When one stumbles upon a holy place, the temptation is to erect a shrine as one departs for home, even as one can never be sure of one's sacred memory. Why are we drawn to an earlier gift, assuming God will recycle the gift, and forgetting that it can never be holy in the same way again? God's good gift of grace is always a transitory revelation.

As a teenager, I didn't know enough about myself, the world, faith, and any relation to them before the summer of 1972. Coming to terms with the soul-truth of who I was, my complex and confusing mix of darkness and light, was first a call to see my ego begin to wither. Prior to the week, there was no room in my life, no space, to consider the art of recognizing there may be more than one faith door to open, that I might travel past many doors, some that open to God and some that open to whatever temptation looks like at that particular time in my life. Would I have the good sense to choose wisely and, beyond that, if I had the power to choose at all, would I open, one day, a door that would reveal the sacred and I would know it?

There are seminal moments that shape and mold how faith plays out. A herd of youth, sandals and legs, wearing bug spray as an intoxicating perfume, gathered after vespers in a cinder-block pavillion, its mortar much too lazy in its effort to keep it standing. Positioned near a grove of scrub pine and shy oaks too fearful of stretching into the Babel sky, the chapel had been designated as a venerable site by a majority of returnees who, despite their flagging holy memories, were willing to sign their names on a spiritual affidavit designating it as sacred. The camp was lakefront splendor and manufactured spirituality for sale to the most sincere apostate of the week. It glistened as a shrine of false prophets and tagalongs for me. After forty years—just about the right amount of time to find some idea of God worth keeping—I named my first confrontaion with God, with lostness, and its accompanying strength.

Looking back, I remember how the oppressive night air made friends with the sweat bubbling in puddles on my sunburned arms. My body trembled as I envisioned the service playing out as tragedy. The service, a last-night-at-camp spiritual free for all, was disturbingly unoriginal; manufactured straw men pulverized before fifty more susceptible scarecrows. I considered leaving, feigning too much sun, but feared that, given my luck, Jesus might choose this night to return a second time and I would be left behind.

I remained seated, my body a paper weight holding down a faint hope the night might be about God or some different idea of God. Maybe God might slip in unannounced and sit beside me, that the night had something to do with me, with my soul's direction, and the naming of the woundedness inside of me. I tuned out the message shouted to me by the preacher hiding behind the plywood pulpit and listened attentively to the young man standing, more pimple than tall, trying to figure out why resistance seemed a blessing.

Manipulation, forever a characteristic of bad religion and church camps, is too often the underbelly of careless faith. It poses as a gauntlet of fabricated piety and emotional double-dare, its status that of a secondary sacrament. The night, as emotionally charged as a July lighting strike, left me frazzled. I doubted every meaningful thought that entered my mind; I did not trust the room or the occasion. The night, its ending predetermined by consenting adults as necessary, summoned me to push down my physical desires. The contract I signed with God in previous years had been declared null and void. It was a different camp with addendums and performance clauses beyond my journal entries which included, pathetically, unequivocal promises I hoped to keep. The cross and thorn combo t-shirts to commemorate my rededication, my part of the contract, sat in brown boxes by the screen door as lamentable door prizes.

How blessed are the misgivings that God spends much time thinking of specific ways to rescue me. I find comfort in that now, but, at sixteen, faith was a contract between myself and God. I knew I could never honor my part of the pledge. My life was not good enough to present to God as collateral. And the camp pastor, the hired gun, worked the room, painting the bleak picture that I was lost and needed to be found. And he played the guitar.

Before God and collective witnesses, he shared, I could promise that I would live differently. Somehow by deeper prayer, guilt, and my soul's flagellaion, I could cast aside my carnal malformations. I stood there hoping my most pious friends doubted his sincerity as much as I did. He presented as needing no one; only seeking rhetorical control over the group. He wasn't dishonest, but possessed what seemed to me the innate ability to make everything he touched wither, spoiling anything that he looked at. I found myself ambivalent toward him; he seemed to be comfortable having conversations with himself. Was the fault in himself, or only in the deep distrust I had for him? A gulf of guilt had opened between us, and we would spend the night looking at each other with eyes that declared a deception suffered. The vital principle of one became a thing of contempt for the other.

That night I felt unfitted for this world, and I knew faintly I was not too good for it and needed some help to discover if I was too bad for it. Something was wrong with me; I needed someone to tell me what. The camp pastor would not serve as the vessel. After many years, I released him from his malfeasance and his inability to take me to God.

The altar call was formulaic, a time of tears scripted at the right places. It was emotional tragedy played out in the shabbiest of theaters. According to the pastor, God's nature was impatience. He stressed the idea of finding God, as if it were a one-time experience and the extent of faith's strength. It occurred to me that God was not the one who was lost, that from the moment I was born God was searching for me. Before any yes to God, God had already said yes to me; before I starting looking for God, God had already been looking for me. I was unable to put that blessing into words or feelings, but it felt worthy of additional reflection.

There was an ugliness to this check-the-box, renewal, rededication, promise that impure thoughts would be removed if I just worked hard enough spiritually to cast aside my carnal nature, that the only sins God really cared about were sexual sins, and that petting in a prayer cabin would make Jesus cry. Ascribing human emotions to the Almighty felt like a bike ride to life-long guilt.

I didn't have a clue about God or a handle on Jesus. I liked Jesus, a lot. He had a record. The Sermon on the Mount was troubling but worth rereading. The camp pastor failed to ask me what life as a follower of Jesus might look like. "Just say the words," he spouted, "the words, I promise," and be sincere enough to want the idea of a personal hell eliminated from consideration.

The pastor was congenial enough on the softball field, dividing our group into teams. That night he separated us again, strumming a tune, a three-chord dirge, while enticing us as a piper leading sheep toward a spiritual cliff. We could jump or beg for mercy. My friends came forward when the pastor gave the invitation. Some of them wept; a few bewildered that they weren't, as if tears were a prerequisite of genuine sincerity. My friends walked to the front. All of them.

I stood at first because everyone else was standing. Soon I realized I was the only one standing. It smelled of poor drama, me waiting for just the right moment to skip forward at the last minute so the flock would be whole, the last remaining prodigal running home without so much as a bawdy story to share. The most important thing was for the flock to be one, no matter how it was joined together. It was ironic that the song we sang was a simple tune that expressed God's love for me, "just as I am."

Adults ministered to the collective, affirming their decision to try again to be better. I knew my friends and cynically sensed there would always be a next fall from grace. But then, how dark was my life, really, my friends' lives? How deficient could sixteen-year-olds be?

The pastor began his personal appeal to me. I felt my pulse trying to escape from my shoes. "Won't you listen to the call of God," he said. "Won't you accept Jesus' forgiveness for your sins," which, I had to admit, were many and too layered to name, but he somehow managed a list: carnality, adaptation to the world's standards, insincerity, and lack of commitment. They were code words and could be interpreted as malignantly as needed. Would I be willing to give my life to God's way? If I had to choose, he said, would I choose to die rather than deny like Simon Peter on the night of Jesus' betrayal? In my high school? Not much chance to die for one's faith. I looked straight ahead, focusing on the piano on the stage, its tune long since dead due to weather variations.

The pastor persisited as if my commitment or lack of commitment reflected positively or negatively on him. He played a final trick: Jesus was going to return soon, the world was in that bad of shape, and like a thief in the night, he would come. Would Jesus find me hiding? Would I be ready? I hoped Jesus delayed his return. I had not had sex yet.

To his credit, the pastor knew I struggled with fleshly desires. I did spend an excessive amount of time with impure thoughts, my sleeping bag concealing any abuse with my hands. But as I remember, there was something hypocritical about adults talking about fleshly things when they could go to bed and be with possibility. These were my thoughts, blasphemous thoughts if shared. Strangely, I did want to follow the Jesus way, but this night didn't feel like Jesus, the way to go, promising something I didn't have the spiritual strength to see through.

It felt like he was missing or ignoring an important point, that surely the Jesus Way was more than sexual purity, that I was being called to make the more difficult choice to give my life to something higher, nobler. I knew I couldn't do it. So, I stood and didn't move.

The pastor kept singing, this time walking toward me, asking me, between verses 9 and 10, to join the others. I shook my head. My friends kept singing; they extended my ambivalence and embarrassment for an additional verse. A youth advisor approached me and asked the same question: Wouldn't I? I sensed she and the pastor were in cahoots. I whispered no. My friends looked at me, staring in disbelief, frightened for me that I would be left out. They urged me to come forward. The flock was incomplete.

There is a moment when, for no logical reason, one chooses to protest, even when the object of protest cannot be named with certainty. No one will convince you otherwise, that you would rather be wrong than admit someone else is right. I felt such. I let myself consider how many times must I repent to sleep well in God's grace? Laying my life on the altar of God, giving my life to whatever God had in store for me, sacrificing my life to whatever God wanted from me. Would God not reveal that to me in a less intrusive way in secret?

The session ended. The singing stopped. My friends returned to their seats disappointed in me, sad that I had not made the night unanimous. It seemed illogical that I was lost to the degree that God couldn't find me in a cabin one hundred yards away. There was a stubbornness involved, something I acknowledge. They could have sung all night, and I would not have come forward. It didn't feel real then. It still doesn't.

I had taken what I considered to be the first step in the purest confidence I could muster. I found the pastor's view of faith to be a dark, narrow alley with a dead wall at the end. Instead of leading to a higher place of joy, the night pushed me downward. It felt earthbound; I had hoped for more, something sublime, that my life might be something more.

It was my distrust of the night and how it played out that darkened the world for me for too many years. I understand that it is an easy sentiment and not easily explained, but the night was so emotionally incomplete. Time, for too many years, would prove vague and thin. More suffering would be needed to reveal it to me as a natural blessing.

The shadows had engulfed the room, and I deliberately, almost malignantly, refused to turn on the lights. I would learn to fight back against the corners of my heart that were impenetrably black. I had wandered among the ugly representation of faith and completely lost my way. Peace, years in the making, would eventually find a place, but I am still haunted by the terrors of that night, terrors which crowd to the foreground of my thoughts as quickly as a home is made for them. What sets them in motion, I pretend not to know.

I love my desert these days. The camp pastor, the chaperones, and my friends pleaded with me to love theirs. They manufactured a desert for themselves and wanted to control my desert experience, especially my return home. They invited me to return to the Egypt of their making, and I had to learn what was so wrong about the Egypt where I was residing. The blessing they believed their desert would give me was not what God wanted to give me.

How thirsty would I have to be to leave their broken cistern? Why not make peace with the imperfect person I am than struggling to become some other flavor of imperfect person? I had to decide how thirsty I was and what I would choose to quench my thirst. All my buckets leaked that night—personal, family, and spiritual. There was no salvation in any of them. Learning to name my leaky buckets required some measure of humility, disturbingly absent from my faith lexicon. That night I felt I had to chance a search beyond all that felt cheap and trivial, that the mud in my soul, while roiling over, would one day settle and I might see clearly again. I remembered something the saddest of all the prophets, Jeremiah, once shared from God: *"For surely I know the plans I have for you, says the Lord, plans for your welfare and not your harm, to give you a future and a hope"* (Jer. 29:11). I would reside in that promise for more than one night and trusting that God was not messing with me.

There will always be a musty smell in my faith home because I continue to seal off the windows to fresh experience, open, ample, and free, preferring the clutter of little shrines, decorations, and mirrors. And idols. My temple is littered with idols, most of which I have collected over the years: ambition, unholy desires, anxieties, and self-promotions. I have been known to haul these unholy things into holy places because they are the cleverest places to hide them.

And some of my idols just happened, forms of faith that possess an initial inherent suppleness, but quickly became calcified and mummified for lack of attention. I choose to keep them close, even as I bow to their hidden destructive forms. All I have to do for holy ground to become unholy is to stop paying attention. Pay no attention to my garden and its an automatic weed fest; pay no attention to my best relationship and see how it rots; pay no attention to the community of faith I serve and witness how deftly it can mutate into a monster. Arrogance walks in. Complacency hides behind. Materialism shuffles in, as does legalism, racism, nationalism, all of them dressed up for their chancel experience. I don't invite them, but I don't have to. It's like a fungus. Any standing institution just grows the stuff, and I wonder if Reinhold Niebuhr's assertion that there are no Christian institutions may be correct.

It is curious, this faith thing. It's not easily had by its nature, and yet I have spent an inordinate amount of time wistful that I can't possess it. I marvel at those who are unfortunate enough to announce its possession with people around to witness. It serves as a shiny bauble for them, and they insist it will wear well in tragedy. I hope for that for them. As for me, faith is strangely familiar. I know I have read it before, even as I encounter it for the first time each day.

I continue to seek a way, any way, to believe that treats my doubt with a modicum of respect; a way that does not demand I give up the hunger in me; a way that does not require me to be stupid, naïve, hypocritical, and conformist; a way that does not insist on an unblemished record of believing; a way that is half-believing memory, somewhere between "Lord, I believe, help my unbelief;" a way that asks I awake each morning and consider the power of the prayer, "Can I break the silence between God and me?" Frederick Buecher speaks of the "in spite of" quality of faith. I rest there, each day, every day. And for reasons I have never been able to pin down completely, it has become my safe home.

Chapter Six

The Darkness is a Map

To go in the dark with a light is to know the light. To know the dark, go dark. Go without sight, and find that the dark, too, blooms and sings. Wendell Berry

There is an uneasy and paradoxical nature of faith, something that David and I talked about repeatedly. We reasoned that faith is more about living excluded than included; more about feeling incomplete than whole; and to our surprise, and salvation, more about being lost than found. Faith, it turns out, is at least the act of learning to name and discern the strength of what we knew to be lesser spiritual paths. We shared how unexpectedly God shows up in our daily routines, in our confusion, doubts, and uncertainty. Despite those who insisted we were dangerously close to crossing over to some side to which we could never return, we chose to chance this new approach to faith.

"Faith presupposes lostness," David shared. "Isn't that what the song says, 'I was lost, but now I am found?'"

"It's the critical line in the song," I said. "Powerful. People know lostness. They know it because they can never measure up to what they imagine God wants. They think of lostness as poor lifestyle choices. Periodically, they may stop their decline. They promise God again that they will do better. They want God to be proud of them, to accept them, and love them again. The underlying problem, the one that pushes people away from God, is theological, always thinking God needs to be appeased. They can't rest believing God loves them unconditionally. They are lost because they can't see God from any mountaintop but Mt. Sinai."

"I once was lost but now am found," David nodded. "I wonder what John Newton learned about his lostness on that slave ship, how lost he really was. He didn't just make one trip, he made many, each time bringing back slaves. He said he repented; he fell on grace. He couldn't believe God could forgive him, but he wanted to believe it. But pastor, Newton had no place to go. I've lived that feeling over and over. I wonder if Newton ever thought about what God would say to him in heaven? Was he sure he was forgiven?"

"I think the word "amazing" is one of the great faith words. There's nothing we can do to deserve it, but we don't trust it. We cover our asses with being good and doing good, just in case," I said.

"I don't have enough time to make my case. No time for additional points," David said as a matter of fact. He didn't sigh with regret or mourn what might have been. "I have nothing to go to God with except my life, my pitiful life."

"It's enough, David. It's enough," I said.

I have spent most of my life lost on multiple faith levels: lost to repeated violations of prescribed ways of living spiritually in this world, handed down and reinforced by those I knew first in my faith journey; lost to indifference and apathy of spirit, that the valleys, of which adults warned would always be close, turned out to be darker than initially promised, and the vistas from the mountain tops, which, while postcard-worthy, have been unable to sustain me for any length of time; lost to self-righteousness and spiritual arrogance, acceding to the sketchy advice from early faith friends that I should model my life around people who self-identified as true believers.

I know true believers; I know people who believe they are true believers. I grew up with them; people huddled up in clusters just inside the church doors like crickets on a change-of-weather day. Upon closer examination, however, they exhibited no real requirement for goodness, no genuine demand for integrity, and no real care for much of anything except their faith superiority. They seemed unaware that the church had become a magnificent place for them to hide. But in their defense, does anyone come to church to be who they are? No, we come to church to be who we hope to God we look like we are. Who could endure coming to church to be who we are?

To be spiritually lost is not the path I would naturally choose. I have always been particularly averse to uncertainty, fearing that any sustained examination of my faith would reveal a more devastating hidden depravity.

I ask myself why I sometimes fear lostness. Because I am beyond the reach of God? Early on, I was taught to live out my faith as a trembling soul—skittish, fearful, and risk-averse—that faith consisted of one dimension—some fanciful promise of some eternal home, and that faith's ultimate goal was to protect that reservation.

A journey without maps, however, a faith beyond my early instruction, is to reconcile my fear of uncertainty with the possibility that God has other plans, maybe better plans, for me. I must eliminate any precondition before starting the walk. Faith, by its admission, is to search for something less secure than what the world promises. If my walk is my own, and mine alone, then I must begin examining the baggage I am presently carrying. Spiritual paralysis is always a safe option; I dare not move lest I stub my life on my first faith's rearranged furniture.

I must let go. Faith resists easy answers or even the answers I think I need. It requires I travel down the corridors of my memories, stopping at places of woundedness and resting there before moving forward. I cannot ask God to change the shape of my woundedness. There is a finality to yesterday that is unalterable. I can, however, ask God to help me change the meaning of my woundedness as I learn to live for my present and toward my future.

David and I were spiritually lost in our particular uncomfortable faith neighborhoods. The power of seeing and thinking of God differently meant at first shifting our focus: Faith was not about being found; we were already found. That was the metaphor that sang of mercy and acceptance from the God we were desperately seeking. Being found was merely autumnal fruit, ripened slowly by God's perpetual insistence to rest in God. The gospel writer, Luke, hints that we do not seek God; God is seeking us, coming forever to us as searching shepherd, or persistent woman, or even a waiting father who spends too much of his day on the porch watching in hope that the shadow in the distance might indeed be his lost son.

I am lost, will forever be lost, and will be lost alone for much of my journey. I have spent too much of my life running from this persistent state of lostness, setting aside the possible strength revealed in lostness for whatever I have imagined as being found. To be lost, however, is first to forfeit any conception that I will one day be found exactly just as I am, while also letting go of any claim that I will be found on my own merits.

I cannot name with any specificity, or certainty, how this new spiritual path is shaping the pattern of my life. At times, I still fear this new path with God; I am still too attentive and drawn to my earlier faith home. How tempting is the call. Repent, rededicate, drone the clergy;

return to whatever others have named as being found, which seems to resemble what they first craved. I find myself disappointed in what they have chosen to pass down.

To be spiritually lost, lost to certainty first learned, asks me to walk past my first spiritual home toward a new home staged with just the right furniture—me and God. It is this new home where I can rest and learn the strength of letting go of the remnants of any spiritual manipulation I have been asked to endure without rebuttal.

David and I avoided any talk of spiritual rules except one: We could never move beyond the reach of God's love. If either of us could sing, it would serve as our faith ditty. In Jesus' parables about lostness—lost sheep, lost coin, and lost son—the idea of lostness is inclusive. Even the ninety-nine sheep were lost in some way, that at some point each would eventually be lost, left to wander in a particular desert, left to wonder if the shepherd, heartsick over one lost lamb, would do the same for them.

"Mother would never agree to such terms," David shared.

"What terms?"

"That God is still searching for me. My being gay is the reason God has stopped," he said.

"Stopped looking? Let her believe what she wants. So, she gets to name when repentance is genuine. She's the one who is lost; she just doesn't know it," I said, irritated that I so easily took sides.

"I'm not going to tell her," he added.

"I will, but she is never going to be in a room alone with me. I feel like a leper around her. She assumes she's healthy and wants to avoid contamination. That, and the fact she doesn't like me."

"She doesn't like anybody. She's not the most beloved of members in her church." He looked up, averted his eyes toward the window as if calling him to something more. "Did you know I've thought about giving her what she wants."

"That you aren't gay?"

"No. Tell her that homosexuality is a sin."

"And that would make her feel better. That would be enough?"

"Probably not. I don't know. I don't know anything anymore. I guess it would be nice to know my mother doesn't hate me. Look, I don't even know why I would want that. I just remember the cold cloth she used to place on my forehead when I had a fever. She wasn't always like she is now. Silly, I know. Remembering that, considering that, wanting that."

"David, she has one song, one verse—you are lost until otherwise informed," I said.

"She's my mother," he shouted. "Do you hear me? I'm going to die without my mother. You stating the obvious doesn't help at all. Why can't you get that? You and Lara and Ruth think this is some game that you have to win. If that's what caring means to you, feeling good about your convictions, then I don't need you."

I wanted to affirm my love for him, but that was not what he needed in that moment. He needed his mother; he needed a damp cloth. I wanted him to feel comfortable residing in their named lostness for him, to live in whatever isolation they had in mind and created for him. I wanted to tell him that the darkness he was experiencing might be the greater gift, that he could never defend himself to their satisfaction, and that they would never be convinced. I wanted to encourage him never to give them the power to determine the movement of his journey home. That's what I wanted to say, but I didn't. I straightened his sheets and kissed him goodbye.

I think about that day when I miss the cues of people in pain. David was right. It had become a war for who would determine the state of David's perceived life. There would be no reconciliation. Those who named him as lost to depravity held fast that there would be no reprieve until they signed off. They were the wounded ones, they insisted, forced to absorb the consequences of David's rebellion into their daily stories. They saw themselves as victims, and that David had inflicted this embarrassment upon their lives without asking.

His parents would determine the intensity of any party or homecoming. And the saddest of days was the afternoon he acknowledged he did not want to be found by them, that he had outgrown his family.

Lostness is solitary by nature. It rarely includes early acquaintances, family, or friends. They cannot imagine a different ending. In Columbus, David stumbled and slept with those with whom he had no prior history. These were the people who first welcomed him with a nod of approval.

"My first faith friends are scared for me," I shared one afternoon sitting at his table, puckish from having skipped lunch.

"Scared that you lost your faith?" he asked

"That I'm close."

"Do you care? I think that's what you shared with me, the same advice," he said.

"You've just been waiting to point out my hypocrisy," I said smiling. "Well, I do care a little. I've only shared some of my faith life with them, but I can tell it bothers them. Why would I intentionally want to upset them?"

"Just tell them you don't believe in God. They will never wonder again," he continued.

"But I do believe in God," I countered.

"I know you do. Tell them you don't believe in God and watch their faces. You can come back with 'just kidding.' Then it will be easier to share what you now believe about God. It won't be as much of a shock. You've taken out some of the sting."

"Their understanding of faith and God doesn't work for me anymore," I confessed to my "whiskey priest."

"And you care about what they think?"

"I do. I shouldn't but I do. I really don't like being known as a fledgling apostate. It feels like a character flaw."

"So, we're both still looking for something that we know only God can give," he said.

"I guess, but it makes homecomings and reunions hard," I protested.

As I make my way without David, I listen to different clues as to what it means to be found on God's terms, in God's time frame. It is possible, I've learned, to be found too soon. When I think of the parables of the lost sheep, lost coin, and lost son, how quickly I have wanted to move to the moment of foundness, forgetting the inherent power of a lost moment, lost time, even lost life involved before any finding. In all three parables, time is a determining factor only in so far as it expresses God's constant searching. How long does the shepherd search, the woman sweep, or the father wait? Until the sheep is found, the coin recovered, and the son returns. Such is God's constant search.

I've found the wilderness to be a fine teacher. The wilderness has never presented itself as a physical place. It's never about geography; I've never worried about dying of thirst. It is necessary isolation without the trappings of what faith looks like as a blueprint, or set of beliefs, or a revelation of God I inherited. It reveals to me as movement toward the holy; its demands unequivocal: the renunciation of illusory projections, the glamour of appearances, the domination of activity, and the autocracy of hypocrisy. The wilderness is an exercise in naming my idols, the idols that specifically deflect from the experience of wonder. The desert is an experience of awe as well as dread and my fascination with both. When lost, when the landscape I have always known falls away or has been taken from me; when what is familiar becomes foreign and I find myself a stranger in the story I once held dear, then I let myself be lost. I learn to rest in that solitary place whose contours I do not know. This is faith's call.

If I spend some days lost, fearful, apprehensive about my new spiritual path, I have to trust it even more, that it is my home for as long as needed. When I am oblivious to the many expressions of lostness, I find comfort that God resides there with me, mindful of the strength and power of what may seem as directionless paths.

To embrace lostness and its accompanying isolation, even to rest uneasily in the consequences proclaimed by others, is sometimes unsettling. There will be those who call my lostness sin, that I have strayed from my faith. And because I refuse to bend to their assessment, they will rest smugly in their conviction that they have earned the loudest word. To offer any defense is futile. David and I learned that painfully.

Resignation is my sad companion. I have resigned myself to the fact than any strength and resolve will always prove too much for those who feel they have the right, earned the right, to name how many ways I am spiritually lost. And I know that at some point in my lostness, those closest to me will stop looking for me.

The family tug is strong and pronounced. They assume they deserve the right to be right about faith, that their sense of spiritual definitiveness is ordained by others in their choir, people who, ironically, are long since dead, whose power is granted only because of the age of fading photographs and hand-me-down stories.

Chapter Seven

The Stranglehold of Preconditions

He who fights too long against a dragon becomes a dragon himself, and if you gaze too long into the abyss, the abyss will gaze into you. Frederich Nietzche

David was realistic enough. His health was deteriorating; the lesions in his brain caused debilitating headaches. He sat for hours on the edge of his bed, holding his head in his hands like a soap bubble. He knew it was now a matter of days or weeks, not months, the outcome inevitable, certain.

"I'm ready, I think," he shared one afternoon, at that part of the day when one begins to consider the questions that will keep one awake that night. "It's slippery, though, walking for so long, trying to be as careful as I can to avoid it for as long as I can. I think I'm ready to fall. I don't want to get up anymore. And I can't prepare anymore."

"That's a prayer," I said.

"Don't quote me. I think I read something similar in Kubler-Ross's book," he chuckled into his hands. "I think I hate her."

"Yeah, she's a real jerk."

"She's just damn right about everything, every stage. I'm just like every other person in this world who is actively dying," he said, "and I wanted to be different, but death makes no distinctions. There is equality with death, and only a few of will be remembered."

"You are not like every other dying person. Not everyone acknowledges the stages of death," I said. "Few people examine their lives as forcefully as you; you never seem to breathe. You are my favorite dying person," I shared through a soft smile. "You're walking around dead and still more alive than most people. But tease me, how many people are you expecting to take part in this great remembering you want? Two? Three? More? People are born, live, and die, and they are forgotten. And you will be forgotten in time, but not now. I may forget you on a Monday, but there will be other Mondays. I will be drawn to something about you, remember something about you, and I won't know why. A song. Your distinctive script. I will think of you, and I expect tears. I will think about how you pissed your life away for a season. I will be angry with you because of what I will miss about you. When you come to me in a dream or a memory, I will be angry again with your parents; then I will return to being angry at you because I'll wonder what we might have been together without your disease. Would we be friends? Would you like me for who I am? There will always be a part of you that will show up when I need you. I don't know if that is enough, but you aren't going to get a monument. But I can assure there will be more than enough people who know their lives have been changed because of you to balance out those who see you differently."

"Will it even matter? David shared. "Trying to go to God should be enough, but I've spent three years trying to be more presentable."

"I believe God is cautious with our stories. I don't think of God as looking for just one or two chapters. God already knows all our stories, is forever saddened, certainly bored, with the way they play out, but it is enough, David. Your life. It is enough."

"I'm going to be pissed off if you're wrong, pastor," continuing to cultivate his annoying pattern of defense when conversations became too serious. For that reason, and many more, our words rarely played out entirely, fully; some emotion always seemed just out of reach, just shy of lovely. "And I won't be sending you any signs that you were misinformed," he said flippantly.

"I only need to be right about one thing," I shared as I picked up my coat and moved to his door. "I just need to be a little right about God. All the other stuff I will leave in God's hands."

"You are my favorite busy body, pastor. I actually think you are nosier than I am. Well, all of you are nosy in your own way. Each of you tries to have the same conversation with me. You take different tacks, but it's the same conversation. Each of you tries to decide which stage of death I am now in. It's a smell in the apartment, the stages of death. It's the fart that lingers. For all that is holy in heaven, has someone put a sign on my back: 'Did David mention dying today? How many times? Who can best address this stage?' Report back to the team and check off another box. And you, pastor, are the least subtle. You just come right out with your questions. No segues, nothing. Didn't your mother teach you manners?"

"She did. She didn't tell me how to talk to someone who is dying, however. I don't think Emily Post has a chapter. Not one word about the subject in seminary. What I wasn't taught is its own book. Too much of seminary is learning to swim in the deep end. Most of the real stuff in life happens in the shallows. In my first church, there was a man who turned on me because I suggested the church not require re-baptizing new members. He shot at me from the weeds for months. I thought that if I invited him to be on the committee studying the issue, he might feel wanted. Big mistake. He just sabotaged me, my supporters, from within. And no one told me that it was okay for me to ask him to leave for the sake of the church's health. Not one practical word."

"What if he gave a lot of money?" David said, adding his own interpretative layer.

"There is that to consider, too," I said, "which brings me back to my hypocrisy? I get some dispensation. It's part of my job to ask questions" I said sitting back down. David wanted to talk more.

"Your job has advantages, pastor. Dying people expect certain questions. What we need is a course on how best to answer the same question with a little nuance. Take Ruth. She's the best. I look at her face and want to tell her everything. And when I do, I get to see her make faces when she doesn't like what I say. She wrinkles her nose and shakes her head. William laughs with me at the absurdity of every day. Evie offers me Raike. I feel like I'm undergoing an exorcism, but I submit because It works sometimes. I don't tell her the demons keep coming back. I also like that she is a closet Buddhist. All of life is suffering, she tells me. I don't think that is particularly novel; it seems logical to me."

"We are a quirky bunch," I shared. "And you forgot about your father checking in. What's that about? He hands you cash for incidentals and never reports it to your mother. I think I could like him some."

"I've always felt that when Dad and I are alone, he wants to be my father," David added. "But together, with mom, accepting me is too much. And he's got to make love to her," he shared casually, almost flippantly, while sipping his Ensure. I sneezed-laughed all over his rug.

"That's an image I can't get back."

"I know. The oddest things come to me. I usually write them in my journal, but I've stopped writing in it. I can't get my thoughts down quickly enough, and my penmanship has gone to shit. I used to think you could serve as my confessor, but I don't see you like that anymore. I don't see you as being able to absolve me of anything that matters. Confession is just so straightforward. Shoot out your shit, promise not to do it again, bingo bango. Pray that one of God's best qualities is God's ability to forget. You don't have the face of a confessor, pastor. Your heart is too involved with your voice."

I can't remember the day when we both gave up on reconciliation. His parents gave no quarter; they remained resolute, walking away from any memory of their son except his future condemnation inflicted by the god of their daily harshness. Compassion and mercy bowed to their insistence and family allegiance measured by decibel levels. Love is forever at odds with our pictures of God. It rarely wins ultimately without qualifications; it spends the night with whatever expression of fear we conjure in our small minds, that resides in our smaller hearts, and dies in its sleep.

Some time ago, I read a statement by Admiral Jim Stockdale, prisoner of war at the "Hanoi Hilton" for eight years during the Vietnam War. "Who did not get out?" he was asked. "The optimists, the ones who said, 'we'll be home by Christmas.' And Christmas would come and go. 'We'll be out by Easter.' And Easter would come and go. By Thanksgiving, many of them had died of a broken heart. One must never confuse faith that one will prevail in the end, which one can never afford to lose, with the discipline to confront the most brutal facts of one's current reality, whatever they might be," Stockdale shared.

Unconditional love, without preconditions, or prejudice, feels like it should be a mark of faith, perhaps the ultimate mark of reconciliation, or at least sisters who share a bedroom without intense squabbles. Families nod in its direction; its breadth, however, is limited to the degree that those who have played by the faith rules feel it is fair. But there is nothing fair about unconditional love.

I spout words each week, tiresome refrains about some ideal about love, and yet, when tested, I am regrettably swayed to seek the safety of my rationalizations. I spend hours drawing from the excuses I have learned and incorporated into years of bad decisions; caught in the trap of judgment that feels so familiar. I hate myself for such feelings, but I am comfortable with what I know to be true. I know that the things I criticize in others are the things I find in myself. Growing up, I entertained the idea of unconditional love in any interim, that time between stolen cigarettes and daily repentance about my impure thoughts, my genitalia in the shadows. I thought I knew unconditional love until I forgot. I felt I was supposed to offer it to the Pryns; I also knew it was painted intimacy, easily covered. I imagined the Pryns and their picture of love etched in stone, fully defined, but never tested for its strength and validity. I gave them nothing but my antagonism, and occasional pity. When authority is in the hands of those who control the flow of ideas, push back is futile. David had to leave home and experience it elsewhere.

We bastardize most faith hints; we mimic unconditional love that costs nothing. And reconciliation begins first in reciprocal hope. To the degree we think we will never be found out, never having suffered under the weight of hoping to receive unconditional love, that our stories will always play out as we have pictured them in our minds, is to walk around dead. And reconciliation dies.

"What happened to your parents when what they and their church named as normal was exposed as a sham? I'm fairly certain it happened, right. I mean, you aren't the only person who ever came out as gay in the church?"

"Who would dare?" David asked. "There are sins, and there are sins. Sexual sins were the worst. And even sexual sins were categorized. Pornography was bad but not as bad as homosexuality."

"So, what did the church do when someone confessed a normal sin? Take me through the process of restoration. At least in their eyes—exposure, first, then some kind of repentance, obligatory confession, seeking forgiveness. Is that the timeline?"

"Sorta," he said. "There is also the season of separation," he added.

"From the church?"

"From anyone in the church. It's supposed to be the time for weeping. Alone," he said.

"And how long did that last?"

"As long as the elders say."

"Anyone ever come back?"

"A few. No gay people, though. I'm the only one. I didn't have a choice about returning. Mother and Dad insisted, and I was fifteen. And when you are fifteen, you don't have a choice, not in the church. It's a collection of stone-throwers. They don't try and hurt you; they throw the stones at your feet at first, but you live under the threat. They can easily aim the stones where it hurts more, do more damage. Just the idea of throwing to hurt is enough to wound. You never come back from that. The people who do come back are the ones who can't imagine their lives forever removed from the church. It's all they know. It's unfortunate. And if they do return, they usually come back harsher and more judgmental. It's now their calling, to name their righteousness. 'This happened to me. This is where I went wrong. I know it. I've seen it, lived it.' It's like they earned a merit badge for participating in life. Everyone gets an invitation into their story. It's like having to sit through someone's vacation slides. You know you just have to endure, nod, and smile. It's hell. I liken it to spending eternity with a recovering addict who has found Jesus as his roomie. That's what it feels like."

There are too many times we cannot bear who and what we are, our contradictions, our hypocrisy. And, too often, faith plays out as fear, fear of having one's prejudices confronted. And so, we dig, mining for souls a little lower than us. Who in our lives must reside on the bottom? We categorize sin. If another is in the wilderness, the degree to which I am also lost is incidental. Someone else is lost. And we believe we can now breathe.

The Moores sat with me in my office. They came to me to express their concerns that David was in charge of our Hot Meals program. The couple had a particular way of looking at life as a personal offense. They implied contempt for everyone except three or four exalted people in their past whom they envied. Everything in their world appeared stained but a small number of ideas of their own.

"He can't be around food," Bette, a retired nurse, shared. "One cut with a knife and everyone is contaminated."

"David is not preparing food," I said. "He greets the guests and sets the tables. He brings flowers and talks to people."

"And you are treating him like a hero," she said, stiffening in the high back chair and positioning herself for what felt like our mutual discomfort.

"It's his way of trying to make amends. But to your point, the CDC says HIV cannot live in the open air for more than a few seconds," I shared.

"The CDC doesn't know everything," she shared dismissively.

"Bette, you are a nurse. You know any risk of contamination is small."

"I know what he does with his dick," she shouted.

I let her words hang in the air. Her fear, bolstered by some first prejudice, supported undoubtedly by her husband in the privacy of their home, rushed to our stage with the ferocity of a charging rhino. At that moment, I felt cold. I saw them now as strangers in our faith community, subversives in our own house. I said nothing, getting no further than thinking afterward of clever things I might have said. Later, I thought about the baseness of her response, the lewdness, the depravity, the ignorance of such a view, and that she seemed to be impressed with the vulgarity of things while, at the same, believing she could keep herself unstained by it.

My mind jumped from accusation to accusation. It appeared as a prominent thought in my mind that night--their brutishness was what they had decided to live for. It was in their soul, not as something to be converted or redeemed, but as recognition of their superiority.

"I think our time is up," I said. "But I want to be sure that I hear you. You are not here because you are concerned about David preparing food for Hot Meals. You've put into words what lives in your hearts and why you are here?"

"We won't be back to church," she said. And they left. There would be no reconciliation, and I let myself rest in the thought that unconditional love is often fraught with blessed consequences.

The stranglehold of preconditions prevents any close examination of what is possible if unconditional love as a method for building and sustaining relationships is entertained for more than a day. How deadly to sidestep the reality that we are an amalgamation of exceptions to every rule, every faith rule. We live in the blessed hope that we will never be found out. If when we are exposed, when what we have named as normal and true and orthodox is revealed as a sham, and when some sort of repentance is required, we reluctantly oblige. We acknowledge our sins and beg for forgiveness. We rest, confident that mercy will be granted because it is always granted. After receiving such grace, however, we now face a more significant threat and temptation to become harsher judges.

There are categories of sins. There are socially acceptable sins, and there are sins like David's that demanded immediate disqualification. Faith rules so embedded, ascertained only from our sacred texts, become so concretized horizons are rarely envisioned. We miss the beauty of the landscape along the road and the relationships made as we travel.

Faith is not a final script, bookmarked for our reference, and divided into scenes that depict life's invasions and certain answers. Faith is by its nature surprising; it is not sacrosanct in sacred texts. Faith resists such limitations. It can never be contained solely in a book whose power wilts under theological emendation. To rebel against destructive interpretations is not to diminish scripture's strength. The movement of the Holy Spirit prods beyond the context of our ancestors. To look for loopholes is to doubt the sincerity of the original scribes. Trying to explain away the horrors and violence found in our texts is to dismiss how our ancestors understood God. The problematic stories within our texts are simply markers that the collectors and scribes were human.

How much of the violence in our world is the result not just of religion but the chosen method of interpretation of sacred texts? How much is the result of our "groupishness," the certainty that my group is all good and other groups all bad? And this divide presents as acts of spiritual violence in which people feel justified to be merciless and unfathomably cruel.

Our sacred writings reveal how human beings once viewed God and found a home for God in such stories. The strength of the stories is not the age of the stories, however. They are frayed manuscripts codified by people who pictured God monochromatically. To posit one's spiritual identity in a set of scriptures only is facile. Whatever voice permeates its pages, we must ask whether the voice's sound and tenor are life-giving or death embracing. And is God, the mysterious, holy other, limited to its pages?

Humanity can never avoid the duality of our natures. We are goodness and hate. Most days evil wins the day. I admit my prejudice and how easily I want and need to separate from those outside my group. I no longer use scripture to justify my biases, however. It's a good first step, resting in something beyond a page. I ask myself if my relationship to God and others enough. Is it possible that what I need to rebel against is a belief system outside myself? It takes little energy not to believe. I've found it takes extraordinary strength and patience to believe as I flit around in my wilderness.

My interpretive lens is fashioned from exceptions. I admit that. "Yes, but," Jesus says, reminding those with an ear to hear that he is the lens by which any sacred text is to be interpreted. These exceptions reveal the precedent for considering extended theological metaphors. Each book of the Bible (my sacred story), my purview, I can find some exception on every page. These exceptions allow me to see the larger faith possibilities when I do not limit God or my relationships with others. What if faith's power rests in what we have received orally—the stories of faith ancestors or contemporaries, in the most benign settings or worse settings?

David once shared that he thought faith was best understood as eavesdropping, listening to the way people have overcome the most brutal of facts, as Stockdale reminds us. What if faith is more potent as a prompt to improvise life and its absurdities. Perhaps faith is making up our lives based on specific gut reactions, clues that can't always be understood or clearly explained. Perhaps faith is best expressed by merely doing. In matters of faith, we first must do, then we will know. We may not be able to grasp the horrors of specific evil, but we must fight against those who would kill because of race. Sometimes faith is pursuing relationships with no thought of what we might receive in return. And maybe our grandest hope is to see the arrogance of assuming we have to be right about faith.

As I stated earlier, David was realistic enough. He wished for more from his parents but refused to settle for a false peace that asked him to bury his resentment. He would try and act out his faith, knowing full well that there would be no blessing, no meaningful reconciliation, his birthright sold off to a better son. He would still live out his life, positioning himself in the family line. He would not be ignored, but would try and shorten the distance between them. The chasm appeared so ominous. I watched him die near the edge, viewing what he had hoped would sustain him in his dying. It didn't.

David was lost by any reasonable measure, spending too much of his life drowning in a sea of lesser places. He reluctantly fell into strength. The trajectory of his soul, prior to his HIV diagnosis at twenty-one, never threatened the stars. How does one become indifferent at seventeen? Is there one event, or many, a series of wounds and cuts so emotionally debilitating that any reconsideration of one's life is thwarted by the intensity of felt pain in the present?

I still have no clue. I do know David sold any thought of a future to anyone who offered even a fraction of compassion to him. He preferred carelessness, expressed in sex.

"I was a sexual predator," he said. "Not children, but I was a hunter, and I was good at it. It was my superpower. My parents at least gave me my good looks."

He shared for an hour one day, offering his pointed analysis of his life as an abuser, that his job, when he held a job, was a means to an end. He worked to fuck, to earn just enough for drinks, which then put him in position to fuck.

He scoured and trolled, growing impatient with regulars at bars, and proudly pissy at perceived slights from those he felt were potential partners. He moved effortlessly among the array of young men just as lost as he. He would reside emotionally in the land of the sinister.

On Sundays, he managed to drag himself out of his nuptial bed for church, leaving his pick up from the night before naked and wondering. To receive his father's check, he would endure church. He would fleece his parents for money, as well as their hope that he would return to them in a more acceptable form, if not emotionally, then spiritually.

There is a decisive moment of recognition when one is dealing with emotional pain when surrender wins, when, in David's case, he ceded whatever remained of his life to death's call. His HIV diagnosis changed everything. The damning pull of possible reconciliation with his family, its inherent strength, bludgeoning strength, determined his move to Seneca. His parents lived there.

"I'm in Seneca for practical reasons," he shared. "I'm dying of AIDS. I have no money, no means of support. What little I get from my family, I need it. I'm dying, but I'd rather not live in a shithole. I have some hope that Daniel and Mary will grieve when I die. I don't think they despise me. I hope they will grieve. Not in front of mother, of course. I guess I'm like any other person dying. I would like to think I will be missed."

David never named the date his mother stopped looking for him, giving him over to his address on Main Street. What prompted David's mother to such blackness of spirit? Did she choose to drown herself in her religious tradition, wading in the only pond she knew? When did she reach that point when she felt comfortable consigning her son to damnation? Are there steps to follow? To consider the plot of damnation is the ultimate spiritual crime. To attribute the opportunity for doing so to the ordering of heaven is madness.

To present oneself to God on such horrible terms insisted she give her son to the levels of lostness not even David ever considered. David's parents abandoned him to his base identity at seventeen. He was brought intentionally to the "far" country, left to fend for himself in the city. She did so willingly and with the assurance that her family of the Book would sustain her decision. These religionists named her as the supreme example of sacrifice, a sacrifice they would never entertain themselves. How impotent this community of faith that David could be found only as a penitent prodigal returning home free from his curse of homosexuality. He would have to acknowledge, confess, his lostness was self-inflicted and not genetic, that re-entry into such a community required his despisement of his rebellion.

Who is really lost? What does being found look like to those who have never considered lostness as soul strife and a necessary part of faith growth? David returned to his family reluctantly, carefully walking around the remnants of what he once remembered as love, a familiarity of love once adorned so beautifully in his memory. He needed whatever he would remember before he came out as gay. He would never ask for their blessing, however. His hypocrisy extended just so far.

I once asked David if there was a moment, an epiphany of whatever God might whisper, something holy and recognizable, that pulled him back toward some gracious light.

"April 19, 1995. That night," he said. I wrote in my journal that "the thing most dreaded was confirmed. FDR talked about fear. He was wrong. Getting an HIV diagnosis is far greater than fear itself. It's even worse than the fear of death. It's the fear of dying and dying badly."

What prompted David to keep looking for an idea about God, any affirmation of God, the day after his diagnosis? What was his first thought after receiving the news he was dying? Did faith have voice, shouting a new theological framework? Was it his childhood theology, presented as judgment, hell, and eternal threat? Maybe it was some of all of these things.

I suspect David found a way to pass his soul to better friends, friends he met at St. Vincent and Covenant. They both were flawed communities, easily manipulated and not above manipulating. They were expressions of group lostness but no one seemed to mind.

Both communities embraced David gingerly for a brief period, but neither possessed confidence there would there be enough time to beat back his family's insistence that his life was incomplete. Any progression toward wholeness disrupted his family's carefully crafted plan to keep his life in check.

Lostness and the accompanying decision to be found never occur in isolation.

Chapter Eight

Imagining God Differently

A bodily disease, which we look upon as a whole and entire within itself, may after all, be but assumption of some ailment in the spiritual part. Nathaniel Hawthorne, The Scarlet Letter

I worshipped at the altar of righteous anger, finding the dance tolerable. I rubbed against certainty, celebrated as truth, but expected more, feeling, most days, as pleased with myself as when rejoicing in another person's joy. I fell prostrate before justice while waiting for God, playing some version of hide and seek somewhere on God's holy mountain, to dictate a social order and vision of the world and how things ought to be—blind, disinterested, non-discriminatory, and as objective as possible. Injustice proved easier for me to name. I knew it when I saw it--naked brutality toward a child of God. I forgot how easily, without constant surveillance, justice can become weaponized justice, castigating and denigrating those who dismissed David and his attempt at a new life.

The Aborigines speak of "dream time," that we are born into dreams, the wellspring of possibilities, subverted only to the extent they are not acknowledged, announced, and explored. What does God look like to those without dreams, those clearly comfortable perishing without them? And what if God, in God's mercy is the destroyer of piss-poor dreams, shattering them, breaking and beating them into submission for everyone's spiritual safety?

David spent hours dreaming of God performing in his journey. "I think I've lost my way intentionally at times just to feel the sensation of a different wind," David shared. "It saved me, that remembrance, the number of times God pulled me back from the brink. I didn't want it to be God, but whispers become breaths and breaths became a breeze. A person has to acknowledge it." In the quietness of the night, he rested close enough to God's whisper.

A part of David was fond of the spectacle that was his life. He could be wildly frustrating, drawing the curtain of his life to me. He refused to share too many intimate details of his sojourn in the city, or offer clues as to the state of his mind during those years. He possessed the infuriating quality of teasing me with salacious gossip and then pulling back the vicarious pleasure. He had no better reason for his silence than that he didn't like to speak about such things except with God.

"Do you think people tell stories in hell?" David shared near the end, when we stopped talking about days of the week and focused on hours of the day.

"Where did that come from? Dear God, take your pills," I shared, laughing, knowing his night had been troubled.

"I wonder these things. Night is my bat-shit crazy time. Put it into a category for me, pastor. There is something wrong with me. I can't shut my mind off. Ironically, I'm sad those thoughts will leave me soon. Soon, no one will care what I thought or why I wrote such boring journals. No one will care. There will be no need for such drivel. I'm sad, pastor. How's that? You think my anxiety pills will help how I'm feeling?"

"How's what? You are all over the map. Which is it, sadness or hell?" I asked. "You started off asking if people tell stories in hell, and then moved to the sadness you will be forgotten. Which topic interests you most, right now. 10:30 am.?"

"Aren't they the same," he continued, "but let's start with hell."

"I don't believe in a literal hell. This life's hell is enough for me," I said.

"I know, but if you did, what do you think people talk about in hell?" he asked. "Do they even talk?"

"Jesus Christ, David, I don't know. If hell is separation, chasm-like, as wide as a hundred canyons, and no emotions, is there anything worth remembering? How's that for an answer? There are no more consequences. Any story of repentance is of no value in hell. Cries can never become stories."

"So, in hell, all interpretation, all reflection, is regret," David said. "Is that what you mean?"

"David, you are not going to hell. I thought we talked about this."

"We did, but last night I wondered why I should trust God to keep his word. If there were a hell, if the images were true—lake of fire, gnashing of teeth, all the cries—then I have questions for God. Where is God as hell plays out? He created it, God's little reminder of poor choices and severe consequences. If God is good, but knows hell, knows the horror, does God walk around with fingers in his ears to keep from hearing the cries? Who could stand that for an eternity? Even God."

"Hell is a problem, big problem if we want God to be good and just," I said. "And I think we have hell because many people have a need for hell to be real. It validates their life, their faith."

"Could you see Jesus descending to hell? Offering a second chance, that when push comes to shove, God doesn't want anyone to perish? That comforts me," he shared as easily as sharing the day looked cloudy.

"It's not talked about much in proper circles. It fits my idea of God searching for us wherever and forever. I just think it would be easier if we didn't have to jump through loopholes to make God nice. You are not going to hell, David."

"I thought about the man born blind, too," he said as he looked at the handful of pills in his hand.

"Hell and a man born blind? All in one night? You were busy," I chimed.

"Yes. I don't think there is a precedent that says I can't have more than one nightmare a night," he countered sarcastically.

"Maybe, but there is a statute of limitations on when you can share it and how many times and to what groups," I said. "It's the stuff of pitch forks and flames, metaphorically speaking; the stuff of accusations and blasphemy. But then why burn a dead man at the stake?"

"The man born blind is my story," he said. "It's never about his blindness, the physical and emotional pain of not seeing. His life is about who is responsible and whose interpretation is going to win the day. Someone sinned, either the blind man or his parents. That's the gossip of the people, the rule of thumb for the Pharisees. And we're still at the same place. It's certainly where I am, someone assigning blame. We haven't moved in two-thousand years. You'd think even the stupidest of people would have been able to manage a few theological thoughts. Nothing changes. It was more important to find out who was responsible than the man's lost eyesight. My parents can't consider my homosexuality in any way other than I am responsible. They have no room in my story except accusations. They think I could pray away my blindness. That's what reparative therapy is, praying away my mistake. It's a short walk to me being a mistake as well."

David and I had no plan except to play around the periphery of his life, taking as our cue his physical impediments. We waved at humility. It did not wave back. We sat in the center of the larger church, in our circle, regarding them, at times, vaguely, resting our eyes on their beautiful blank faces, and bewildered that the fertilizing dew of the "least of these" descended too seldom on their spirits. We did not judge them harshly or publicly. They were aware of something wrong, something ugly, but we served as a parenthesis, a chapter to ourselves, blank pages waiting and watching, learning on the fly, and there was no more time or room for justice to play out with any new friends as per David's directive.

"I can't have any more friends," he shared as he marked off another day on the calendar with a marker. "I can't tell my story to another soul. I don't have the energy and, honestly, I don't want to. I know it sounds horrible, but I can't. You'd think I would welcome anyone who might extend mercy, but I can't. I look at my life. Jesus, it's a soap opera. I know some peace, feel it at times, but I just can't break any more hearts. I can't."

Justice is not always blind and dispassionate. Jesus seemed willing to state upfront, to the embarrassment of his closest friends, that justice is found in the extravagant invitation, expressed forcefully in one of his most disturbing parables about a supremely gracious boss and workplace fairness. "Come, everyone, I'll show you what is right and just. And just for fun, I'll show you the breadth of how extravagant I am by paying the last one first."

As a person who desperately wants to believe, I pray and preach and read and write, but something has always been missing. I hold conversations with myself, oblivious to the fact that God has sent regrets, that God will have no part in unidimensional justice. For the times I've wanted to give up on certain people, I can't because of confrontational parables about a God who doesn't; who, as the protagonist in the parable of the gracious boss, keeps burning the pavement back and forth downtown, relentlessly determined not to knock off work until everyone is treated right. Such extravagance included David's parents, Peter and Nora.

When I return to my pages, the notes of rage and dismissal written ten years ago, my contempt for them, I now realize how seamlessly justice became tyranny toward David's parents. I removed any consideration of love and compassion extended toward them. Justice became my understanding of justice which, ironically, looked and tasted like a side dish of their particular judgmental theology. I embraced an ideology I professed to deplore, intoxicated with trying to win moral and theological skirmishes by ambushing them whenever I could.

It was a conceited time for me, self-important, a time for all seasons and emotions. It was a time of grace, as David extended it, and it was a time for throwing stones; it was a time to run roughshod over the histories of people who first presented as assholes. It was a time when one story became the only story.

My faith, captive to secular dogmatism, protected me from the exclusion of religious tyranny. I intended to follow the Jesus way, a model worth my time and energy. How impotent to spend one's life seeking bankrupt analogies without possessing the courage to make a stand and farming God's universal field with a backscratcher.

There was nothing courageous about my decision to reach toward David. What was I risking trying to protect David? Disapproval? Isolation? What was particularly courageous about a stance without underpinnings except for choice? I woke to a dawn and flung myself in the direction of friends who shielded me from the pain of sustained introspection.

Courage is a faint odor, a whiff of something I am called to develop rather than watch unfold. When I mature by reconfiguring myself apart from the titillations of faith's promised rewards, when I overhear myself talking, whether to myself or to others, when my words hang in the air for what seems to be an interminable period and I consider pulling them back, I have chance. When I catch the glimmer of tears in the eyes of the person I wounded, I am a real boy. Self-hearing is the royal road to redemption when I listen to my inner prejudices and to be willing to suffer change. Real courage is risking my tired theology, taking respite from language, any language, but especially language about God. It is possible to be wrong, maybe not at the moment when injustice appears visible, but in the aftermath, when bodies are counted and bagged. I failed, not just in trying to protect David; I failed in love and love's considerable extensions.

"What if my parents have been wrong about God?" David shared. "What if they've been wrong about me? What do I do? If they are wrong, but I can't convince them they are wrong, what do I do with them? Consign them to whatever hell they have imagined for me? There's a part of me that wants them to know such torment—a purgatory of their own making. But Jesus keeps getting in the way. That's why I decided to create my wall of imperfection."

"I think I like the wall, but I have questions. I've drawn some conclusions, my interpretation," I shared.

"I take a magic marker and write their names on the wall," he explained. "I can't lose them there. I sleep on my side facing the wall. I can see their names, just below the curtains. The light will eventually shine on each name. I can't pretend they don't have a place in my life. I have to deal with them, all of them. And I have to deal with myself and how I feel about each one of them. I have to deal with my anger toward them and how easily it can win out if I'm not careful. Pastor, have you ever prayed for your enemies? 'Love your enemies,' Jesus said. He may have been on to something. Try praying for someone for any length of time while trying at the same time to keep your heart from that person. It can't be done. Something changes in you."

When I remember David, I realize how inattentive I had been in those final days at what he considered—a new faith revelation. I cringe at what I missed. I resented him for it, and how he forced me to think well about this truth and whatever truth I could sustain without perishing. On several pages in his journal, David hinted at the reciprocal pain he shared with his parents.

"No one faith expression is noble at its core, not my parents, and not mine. Our beginning assumptions shape how we live out our best or worst. Faith will always be a solitary walk. Tonight, I hope to decide if it's worth the effort to walk alone. I am tempted to let others struggle for me." Two weeks later, he wrote:

"We spend so much of our lives broken by those we have loved first in our lives. Families wound as frequently and as severely as the most pernicious enemy. My mother does offer pie after she knifes you, however. For the life of me, I don't know why I stay within earshot of people who will not or cannot come around because of religious objections. I have to know why. I will continue to speak their names each night, hoping for an answer that will help me not be afraid to die alone." And explaining his wall.

"My prayer wall is a reminder that, before I sleep, I must whisper to God all who are in pain, some in more pain than me. It also reminds me the world doesn't revolve around David Pryn, although there are friends who would offer a rebuttal. Some hurts cut much deeper than my disease. I have to include Peter and Nora in my prayers. I have to."

"You can't let your parents go, and I can't let my family go," I said one evening as we put his groceries in his cupboard.

"From what you've said, you might be just as messed up as me," he shot back.

He was right. For most of my life, I have envisioned a picture of family in my mind. But now my family has become peripheral; I can't imagine my family except superficially. I can't pretend they can be for me what I need as I make my way differently. I am not better for it, far from it. I have siblings who possess the softest of qualities, sincere expressions of what they envision as love. It works for them. Each of us manages our lives differently these days, trying to rewrite our stories in a more favorable light. My parents had their demons that strangle raw emotions. Their demons no longer had to work for control; my parents ceded to them willingly.

I knew David's parents superficially. I met his father once in passing one afternoon when he brought over food. I wanted to despise him; I hated the way he and his wife treated David. Their brand of Christianity was abhorrent to me, their smugness infuriating. There was nothing they could teach David now, no letting him make mistakes and suffer the consequences. Their son was dying. The Pryns, each of them Adam and Eve in the morning, knew no time when they were not who they were now—self-created, their strength, and power their own.

"My family is close. Two blocks. Your family is hours away. But, pastor, I'm going to die without my family near me in any meaningful way," David shared, "and they live just down the street. I've already let them go, at least emotionally, but I'm still drawn to their faces, the light in their eyes before I came out. I remember a time when they were loving and kind and mistaken. After I told them I was gay, I became a problem to solve. And they stepped back from me. They didn't have the right tools to fix me. I'm going to die without my family. Think on that. Anything sadder than that, pastor? You may be the only one with me at the end, and unless you say something meaningful at my service, I will be a footnote."

'I have three children,' my mother will say, 'Daniel and Mary live close, and David died young.' That's my legacy: I died young. I can't do anything about it. Mother gets to write the last chapter. Mother and Dad can't come to me softly; they can't smile a gentle smile. If they have regrets, I will never know. I don't expect anything from them, but I'm banking my life and my eternity that you can't love like Jesus without tears."

His had been a thirty-year sojourn in and out of the nothingness of his family's desert. The piercing cacophony of voices in the interior geography of his heart reverberated throughout his memory. For most of his adult life, David had wandered alone, meeting his family at specific holy sites and on holy days, where ambush was as predictable as the Sunday brunch menu. There was something to be learned, even in church, he reasoned, if only what to avoid.

When I knew him, David desperately wanted to be free his parents, the two people he once assumed wanted to save him unconditionally. They were never up to the task. He suffered melancholy at what might have been if faith and God were eliminated from their stories.

"They can't get past the only thing that matters to them. I'm gay. Pastor, have you ever thought that where you interrupt a conversation determines if a future is possible? Mother kept telling me that "the wages of sin is death," highlighting the verse in her over-sized Bible. It felt like she was compensating. That's all she shared that is worth remembering. I think back and laugh that she assumed that my being gay would be the worst thing that could happen to me. I would say to them, if they wanted to listen, 'I will be dead before you, yes, but only for a season. You, too, will be dead soon enough. And then we will all be dead together, for eternity. And what will we carry with us into whatever eternity means? Grudges? Indictments? If those things don't matter in God's eternity, then why do they matter now? If forgiveness is a given in God's great homecoming, why do we have such a hard time considering it now? What if, in God's good grace, I am granted occupancy in heaven? What if heaven is all of us living in the same neighborhood? What if, in heaven, I get access to their gated community? What if they can't avoid me? What if the jerk in me drops by every day for coffee and doughnuts?"

The Pryn's wounds represented several generations. His mother may have suffered; his father may have suffered as well. Neither knew a different way out. They would never be able to name, much less look after the wounded child in themselves. How could they possibly save David?

David would keep his fragile soul, broken in his mind and heart in just the right places, and for what he believed to be the best of reasons—to break the damnable spiritual cycle. Condemnation and destruction could not be a part of his struggle, could never be presented as the right solution. He would look to creative mercy, which eventually included mercy to himself. Tragedy begets tragedy, forever and ever, until someone summons the strength, the courage, and the understanding to say, "Enough!"

Chapter Nine

Finding Better Friends

The inherent danger in creed, in belief over faith is that belief is passive. Faith is active and leads to discipleship. Creed or belief, simply requires recitation. What is the point of believing a whale swallowed a man unless we understand it is a story about justice? Will Campbell

David flitted back and forth between several religions, rarely lighting for an extended period. His search for meaningful faith included a hodge-podge, pick and choose medley, whatever fit his soul at that moment. It was never the church itself, but the community that won his heart.

After he came out as gay, he attended services off and on to please his parents. He tempted them each Sunday with his possible conversion.

"It was cruel what I did," he admitted. "The one thing they wanted was for me to confess. I refused. I don't think I consciously said or did anything for them to consider I might change, but I was still a shit. My presence at church planted and watered whatever it was they hoped for me. I guess they gave the Holy Spirit too much power."

"Well, so we are entering the world of blasphemy," I said, grinning, his biting wit enjoyable.

"Which part?" he asked.

"You know which part," I said.

"I'm not taking shot at the Holy Spirit. I believe God can and has changed me in so many ways. For years, I used people—for money, for sex, for position. I made friends based on what they could do for me and what I could get from them. I was a manipulator. God has forgiven that part of me but not my homosexuality. I don't need God's help with my identity," he said confidently, even defiantly.

"I've been through reparative therapy twice. Mother and Dad put me there. I hated them for it. I knew what they wanted me to give up. They promise too much, these places. They shouldn't be allowed to make such promises to kids. And most of the leaders I listened to had their own demons they were trying to hide," he said.

"If your beginning assumption is wrong, then any conclusion is wrong," I shared thinking how silly my support sounded.

"Those places are not only wrong, they are mean," he said. "Mean to put kids through that. I know. I heard the stories late at night. Kids just like me, wondering, afraid, kids who grew up with God. Well, some idea of God, or their parents' and preachers' ideas about God. You know, the people who read the Bible like a lawyer, looking for verses to make their case. They piss on joy and love and mercy. But to your point, I don't think the Holy Spirit gives a tinker's damn about changing something in a person God has already put in place. I was created gay and the Holy Spirit doesn't care."

David was Church of Christ first, the church of his parents. As a child, he heard the stories and the commentary. The stories did not possess the power to move beyond a particular context. There was one meaning and interpretation, and this method would be used as the first step toward David's victimization, his first experience with biblical "insistence"—one meaning, literal and damning.

Before finding Covenant, he attended St. Malachi Catholic Church. They welcomed him, assisted him in practical ways. And David, ever the manipulator, weaseled a burial plot in the Catholic section of the local cemetery out of the priest. The church held in reserve the one thing David needed most, collegiality. Their love had a price tag, however. They loved their neighbor, clothed their neighbor, and still rejected their neighbor as their neighbor.

"Why, Catholicism?" I asked. "They aren't known for welcoming gays," I said, my eyes darting back and forth to the number of saints David had nailed on the hallway wall.

"I think I just love the icons and rituals," he said.

"That's it? That's all it takes to win your allegiance, some wall hangings? You are a cheap convert," I smirked.

"I love them because they remind me of religious soldiers. I like to imagine them in strategic locations around my bed, protecting me from harm. I'm a spiritual whore. I will take any expression of love, anything, really, because I don't want to die alone."

"Catholics do have a lot of saints," I said.

"I know. I love it. Name a problem, a concern, and bingo, there's a saint to help, someone to pray to, someone to take up the cause," he said.

"Kinda creepy," I said. "I don't want anybody hovering over my bed, all those dead people watching me sleep."

"Yeah, I know it's silly. It works for me. You think God is present with me all the time. I believe that, too, but I like covering my bases just in case St. Anthony has an in with God that I don't have. I like the rituals because I don't always know what to say to God in every circumstance, and the Catholics seem surer about these things. The rituals let me get away with not talking to God in a meaningful way when I'm angry."

"So, anything to help you die with some assurance?" I pressed. "A naked Christ on a cross? The pull of confession? It sounds like you are trying to cover your ass with Mother Mary as your savior."

"I need a wad of grace in my hand as I go," he said. "I can't let go of this feeling I have that I need some punishment before I go."

We sat for a while. I offered nothing. Tears puddled in the corners of my eyes; they never flowed. He looked at me. Kisses seemed to jump from his eyes, eyes that I knew could not look upon people without wanting to drape people in passionate caresses, even his family.

It was funny. His search for acceptance in religion did not look much different than his search for approval with his family. He would feast on whatever crumbs he found under the communion table or his mother's antique buffet.

For the rest of his life, he held out hope for his father, a torn, conflicted man, who loved his son enough to write him a check for expenses, but not enough to invite him to come back home. David stopped hoping for anything from his mother. She determined the depth and frequency of love extended. Both of his parents possessed no capacity for change; their curious blindness dominated them until David's end.

There is a danger in entering a person's story late when the plot's shape has been revealed early and often. David had AIDS. He loped into our lives in oversized slip-ons, shuffling rhythmically near the corners of our prejudices. Some at the church felt he was a test case about our willingness to address the weeds in our spiritual garden. He shared about his life, his mistakes, his defiance, and the consequences of his bad choices. He stood before us one Sunday and let us peek into his medicine cabinet and his soul.

"I take 78 pills a day to stay alive," he stated almost matter of fact.

"What's the most difficult part of your day?" a church member asked.

"The hardest part is at night, one or two in the morning when all the church angels are gone. I try to sleep, but it's too quiet most nights. I am alone with God, the saints, with my thoughts about what is happening to me. I think about crazy stuff. 'So, this is what dying is like.' Most nights, I don't sleep. My mind won't shut down. But then I look at my wall with all the names of my church family. The light from the streetlamp shines through the window and on the wall. That's how I go to sleep—here in my bed, but also in my church."

Were that haloes a more reasonable price. His suffering was just that, only that, suffering. He managed his life with a modicum of grace, but his suffering would never go gently into his night. As we watched him wither, he became more than our cause, which is always the most boring of spiritual practices.

Covenant United Church of Christ sits on the corner of two imperfect streets, sullen brick roads carrying people to their perfect unhappiness. The church is post-card worthy. It is also an architectural money pit, hampered by history and designations from societies. Early in the twentieth century, the framers decided to cover the soft, porous brick with pasted stucco, now as splotchy as an eczema outbreak. The building's front is weather-worn, attracting in the summer humidity the friendliest of mold cultures. At first glance, the front of the church is imposing, possessing a somewhat incommunicative character. The front, however, is the mask, not the face of the church. Its function seems less to offer communication with the world than to defy the world to speak for them. A three-foot-high black-iron fence, positioned for decorative purposes, lines the sidewalk that runs parallel to the church, revealing, at least, the church's serious aesthetic indifference to charming beauty. On the South corner, there is a bench, a lounging place for one or two who wear the air of the undervalued.

The church possessed a rich history because, in its estimation, the community of faith was on the right side of history. Founded on anti-slavery and temperance, the church rested on competing poles, justice and alcohol, which meant the church championed justice but rarely raised a glass in celebration. The church's firmer natures were those that shone at the larger times in its history, including the rumor that it was part of the Underground Railroad. There was no evidential proof of the story's validity, but the church believed it could be true, and lived out their ministry as if it were true.

The church named injustice more than once in its two-hundred years. "It's what we've always done," said Joseph Beckwith, church member and town's librarian. "We've never lived off the suffering of victims long since dead. Wherever the church saw injustice, we responded, usually once a generation. We've been the nigger church, the feminist church. Now, we are the gay church. Kinda makes one proud, doesn't it?"

I first saw David leaning against the lamp post, his left hand caressing the pole with an almost imperceptible gentleness, his fingers as gray as the silver metallic paint on the pole.

"I have to rest regularly," he would later admit. His mind stabbed the nerves in his feet, numb from neuropathy, to move; he spanked the floor with his mis-sized shoes, Birkenstocks he stumbled upon at a used clothing store. It became evident that Covenant would serve as his final stop, the last church that might consider nobility as a caption for his life. We were part of his "foundness" game plan. He needed God, but he wanted a beloved community more. Would our church play with grace? Would he live long enough for him to feel we absolved him of his life's debts?

David ended up at Covenant because of our ministry to the poor—a meal, a Hot Meal, offered each Tuesday. We partnered with our friends from St. Malachi, David's spiritual home before Covenant. I was introduced to David by Jack Raabe, who had come to Covenant via the Lutheran church, a community of faith who loved his energy but was unwilling to love him as a gay man.

"They were always inconsistent," Jack shared, "and I got tired of trying to justify their spiritual homophobia." Each year he waited for his acceptance letter from the bishop, even a note of acknowledgment from the synod that his life was recognized and named, that he was of value and not being used. It never came.

Jack and David became easy, comfortable partners, each bringing their different gifts to bear on the church's ministry to the poor. Like a carnival Catholic, David preferred rituals, even breaking bread with the nimbleness of a veteran priest.

"Rituals have sustaining power," he said. "It's their nature, rinse, repeat, and rinse. The repetition brings magic to people. They know how they are going to be received each week—with dignity and compassion. They don't have to worry about some rule that makes them feel wanted or unwanted. Love has no terms."

The formal meal became eucharistic almost immediately. Subtle and not so subtle adjustments were implemented. "No more plastic forks and paper plates," David instructed. "We have a commercial dishwasher. Let's use it. I've eaten in church basements, too. Plastic tells those who gather, those who are hungry, that they don't matter, that the meal is nothing more than drive-by. No more moveable feast or styrofoam plates. No more serving yourself."

David seemed to be free-falling toward grace and whatever zirconium studded crown awaited him in heaven. He welcomed the gathered pain that pooled in the social hall on Tuesday nights. Guests arrived early, around four-thirty. The fellowship hall had been painted milky-green, a color never imagined on any color palette. White bookshelves filled with books, the right books, popular books, and the correct faith books lined the walls. The library, funded by an endowment gift of R125,000 by Amy Williams in 1953, allowed the church the freedom to codify its theological position. The indoor-outdoor carpet in the social hall was spotted with ministry mishaps. The Hot Meals guests nodded to each other, men and women who recognized each other from other social agencies in town. They saved seats for family and their closest friends. It was elementary school cafeteria exclusion. Their only password? Family pain.

David side-stepped the judgment of those who felt the church was merely enabling the guests. It was always a mist that hovered too close to the ministry. Some in the community affirmed the ministry but wished the guests were more accommodating of protocol.

"They smoke on the front steps," one member criticized. "The church is more pool hall than a sanctuary."

But then there was Manny from Portugal, a sweet fundamentalist who found Jesus late and wanted to make up for lost time. He served as chaplain for the group. He dreamed of being a minister but resigned himself to bringing prayer—rapid-fire, coded, a second language, sharing his deepest and often too personal revelations which prompted repeated elbows from his wife. He managed to give each of us something to take with us—a boxed blessing for later consumption.

David pilfered the room with his long-suffering. He bathed in his need to be noticed, and people splashed just enough affirmation toward him to keep him upright. He tended to flitter from table to table like a moth drawn to light. He moved purposively, touch and go landings on asphalt too hot for any lengthy visit. He smiled, acknowledged, and encouraged, superficial mutterings while searching for the back of the next metallic chair to hold his weight. He extended whatever grace he could muster, each guest given thirty seconds, just enough time, he reasoned, to keep complaints to a minimum. And strangely, despite his compassion, some of the guests were quick to judge his homosexuality.

"They are no different than the rest of us," Ruth shared. "They just happen to be poor and prejudiced."

I reread an article David wrote for the newspaper about the church's Hot Meals Program. "The Mount Vernon Hot Meals has been going strong for eight years now with the cooperation of multiple congregations. It's more than a food program; it's a ministry of love and compassion. The meals are for those who are hungry for fellowship, for conversation, for love. If your stomach is growling or your heart is aching, you are welcome. These daily meals are times of communion for all involved. Whoever is kind to the needy, in whatever form, honors God."

The fellowship hall was set up each Tuesday. White cloths covered each table. The church's china, used sparingly and for larger and grander events, dotted the round tables. Candles and flowers were fashioned into acceptable centerpieces.

The eucharistic meal would play out as a meal Jesus might attend. It would be available to all, shared by guests and servers, in what we imagined as a heavenly banquet.

Chapter Ten

The Wilderness is an Acceptable Graveyard

To move wild laughter in the throat of death? It cannot be, it is impossible: mirth cannot move a soul in agony. Shakespeare, Love's Labour's Lost

The tile in the room, winter white, flecked in an indifferent gray, requested an audience. I scanned the floor for a pattern. I intentionally averted my eyes from his corpse, the way one knows something or someone is eerily present in a room but fearful of confirmation. I managed only small thoughts when I glimpsed his frame—the stubble of his beard too much for his weary face. There was an indecency to his face. Even the most beautiful of his features surrendered to death's insistence. In my mind, I pictured his eyes, once so piercing they could damn weak souls to silence, now open, as vacant as his life. I attached my eyes again to a spot on the floor as if I were making a strong effort to say nothing but what I ought.

David's life challenged the incongruity of my interpretations. Reading between the lines of his life was always easier than following the text of his life, however. I took for granted I would be able to write him in bigger letters. He felt vibrant the week before, ready to meet the requirements of my imagination. "When people forget I have AIDS, I am inconvenienced, but it's worse when they remember it," he shared days before he died, choosing his words almost as a prelude to something grave. He knew the sounds of words before he knew the depth of their sting.

Death advances the way death advances, practically, enthusiastically, giving too little time for better memories. David had danced in the light of the nearest star, its dust enough for his meager dreams. I now watched his magnificence grow cold. How easily I had made him an idol, his story looking for the ending we both knew would never come.

"You expect too much of me," he said the last time we spoke in person, having been admitted on Monday, late in the afternoon, with headaches so severe he was vomiting blood.

"That's fair. I do expect a great deal from you," I shared.

"I will disappoint you, always," he mumbled while turning to find a more comfortable position in his bed.

"My expectations of people have survived disappointment," I said, trying to amuse him, as if he should be happy enough to fake a grin. Instead, he smiled at me as if the Madonna had kissed him. Tears puddled in my eyes. This time the sting suggested to me the slipping of life.

"I love you," I said, revealing an awkwardness but none of the oddity of sharing it in a hospital room.

"Keep it," he said. "Keep it until the end, for later." We continued to talk as if there would be later. We succeeded in making the idea appear almost just. David did not allude to his death being near, but we both knew he would not outlast the summer. The reality was enough, distinct without having to erect signposts in our conversations.

"I won't have a chance to say goodbye to the angels," he said.

"I can arrange for all of us to come to the hospital," I said trying to save the awkward moment for a more suitable time of manufactured emotion.

"Let's keep that for a final pleasure," he said.

These were final thoughts, both of us knowing the truth but unable and unwilling to share it completely. There is nothing drearier than a last interview, nothing so emotionally self-serving than remembering emotions not present except in one's imagination. One never says the things one wants when death is close. The tendency as years pass is to add rather than delete. Conversely, one usually says many things one shouldn't, only from a sense that one has to say something. There is something blessed about the ability to revise our muddled memories at a later date.

David was still lucid on Tuesday, the day of my visit. He was the last of my pastoral calls in the city. That afternoon, he created for me an opportunity to draw a slight breath, relieving me of heavy responsibility, for in that room, I was empty. I possessed no light to spare from my small reservoir.

The night he died saved me, but it would be years before I would receive it as a map toward any dawn. It is strange the invasion of obscure thoughts and patterns. I remembered a piece of a poem I was writing when I received the call from his nurse telling me his death was imminent. "Soon," she had said. I want to remember the conversation including more. Surely there was an introduction, but her name to this day still escapes me. "On wings aloft, I strain to reach the heights necessary to glide on the fiercest of winds," I repeated as I hung up the phone and walked to my car to drive to the hospital. It served only as a line in a poem, the latest self-absorbed companion piece to my latest journal entry. I wished it to be a worthy prayer as I tried to intercede to God on David's behalf. Would these fierce winds ever present to me as a means for soaring?

The time of his death recorded on his death certificate was nine twenty. David was dead before I got on the elevator at the hospital. His death was unworthy of cinema, but then we had lived our goodbyes for three years. I opened the sliding door to his room, and the nurse motioned me in.

"Stay as long as you like," the nurse whispered. I stood just inside the room, choosing to watch her declare David dead from a distance; I watched her unpack the pockets in her smock—lip balm, body lotion, a comb. She reached for a basin and washcloth. Carefully she bathed and anointed his body, extending the comb through his matted hair, stroking his face as if summoning a genie, and attempting to return his features to a softer gray. I slumped in the chair next to David's bed, paralyzed by what was now in front of me, what was now my necessary final task.

I remembered the nurse. She was a woman of considerable weight, pear-like hips that she managed with ease, shifting, floating, like a ship's cargo stowed carelessly. We had exchanged names outside David's room after one of my visits, but I had side-stepped her presence, fearing what she might reveal without any inquiry from me.

"Do you have people to call?" she asked, prompting me awake from my dullness and sedentary heart and mind.

"I want to call Lara," I mumbled.

"Is she a friend?"

"And more," I shared, "She'll tell me to get off my ass, make the call I have to make, and come home."

"Anyone, really. The funeral home?"

"I need to call Brent. He will send the ambulance tomorrow morning. I assume you have a morgue."

"Basement. I can call now if you like," she said.

"I need to ask his parents what they want. Don't like thinking of David staying overnight on an ice tray."

"Doesn't matter to him," she said. "Look, David thought you could handle this, or you wouldn't be here. You are the only one on his contact list. Time to do your job."

"The two people I have to call are not the people I want to call," I protested.

"If it helps any, his parents visited yesterday. I've seen them here at other times. Felt perfunctory, but they showed. Call them."

"It feels like they won," I said.

"I don't know anything about that," she said staring at me.

"They feel like David got what he deserved," I said.

"We get a lot of patients like David. They look alike. Young. Gay. It's a club. They come here because they have no money. They come. They die. A few friends visit. They come. They fade. I do my job. I don't think about punishment. I think about sadness, the waste. David was demanding as any patient I've ever had. But he was grateful for the least little extra care. He was tired; he was ready, but he didn't know how to let go. I assume that's where you come in."

"We talked a little about dying, what it would feel like," I said. "Mostly we avoided it. We laughed about how absurd it is, dying. He talked about how surprised his parents will be when they get to heaven and see him there."

"I don't believe in God, "she said, speaking the imperative as easy and as carefree as if commenting on the size of her shoes. "Well, I believe a little, but Christians give me a headache. I see parents at their worst, trying to find some place to live around their son, wanting to love their son, even, but they can't because of, well, God. I watch their faces when they visit. Sometimes I don't even know if they have a religion, but you can feel their judgment, their discomfort, their inability to love their child just because he is their child. I've seen mothers keep their coats on the entire visit; I've seen fathers holding up the wall in front of the bed, as distant as they need to be. Why did they come? One kiss, one kiss on the forehead, a half-smile, even a forced smile, would mean everything. And God gets in the way."

"I'm glad they visited," I said. I didn't mean it. I cringed when I said the words, their aftertaste as bitter as any unsourced herb. I offered them too cheaply without thinking, but it fit my life's pattern to make things easier and more comfortable for everyone. I thought of all the times I had misspoke simply because death had entered a room.

"Well, that's not true," I added as a qualifier. She listened as one who listens while attempting something more important. "Let me revise what I said. I want to be glad, but I still want to hang on to why I don't like them. They didn't deserve him, and they don't deserve to know he's dead." It's never too late in the day, or too late in life, for bitterness to fall asleep in justification's arms.

As we talked, I realized I was now standing, prowling, pacing my emotions as stealthily as a predator. I found myself outside David's room, having ended my conversation with the nurse without so much as a nod that I needed space. In the hallway adjacent to the nurses' station was a waiting room and coffee. I considered tea but poured coffee. A husband and wife sat in the room. I can only assume a husband because who would make such grand gestures if only dating. The man gyrated with arm movements, and the wife nodded affirmatively, calming him publicly if for just a moment. He did not appear violent, but there was anger in his first impression. I am not very exact at measurements, but it appeared to me that if the wife pulled herself up, she would be the taller of the two.

Returning to David's room, I paced around his bed, this pitiful site that would become as holy to me as any memory of any shrine I ever knew. I shuffled from his bed to his window. I considered praying, but I knew it was not my strength. I had always assumed too little regarding prayer. I choked out what felt like honesty to me, acknowledging the deep divide that I had created as a precis to any of my prayers. I attempted to break a silence between us.

I had been preparing for this moment. I had prayed that I would be with David when he died. I thought I was ready, forgetting this is also how a family dies. I reached for my phone, scrolling my contacts, pausing long enough to realize my inattention to so many people who touched my life. Pryn, Peter. I didn't remember typing his name into my phone.

I called David's father, and I shared the news abruptly. I muttered that David was dead. I offered no preface—'I'm sorry, your son is dead'—the sweeter, softer amenities. They felt so underserving.

"Don't leave," he said. "We are on our way." To this day, I don't know why he asked that of me. We were not close. We tolerated each other when, in those infrequent times, we were in the same room. I assumed he did not want any spiritual comfort. His use of the collective pronoun surely meant Nora Pryn would be coming as well. My mind began to envision scenarios, none that were grand or kind or merciful. No one changes courses without thinking about the perils of the adjacent terrain. The moment of death offers a false construct.

"Are you ready for this?" I said to David. "Your mother and father are on their way. This is not how I thought the end would play out. I imagined it would be just us. But then nothing has worked out the way we hoped. We have to have one more conversation. Let me do the talking. I promise, David, I will protect you."

The Pryns walked into the room, followed by a number, greater than ten, of people posing as a posse--the villain, dead on the bed, their biggest regret. They had come with their unhappiness when the night, at least for me, felt complete. They appeared like people who would do their best to darken the brightness of pure rays, men and women wanting affirmation that their unhappiness could not have come through their own fault. They looked small to me, like witnesses scurrying from behind the curtain of an execution chamber wanting to see the face of a dead convict. Their presence conjured an image in my mind of preliminary music before a healing revival.

Letting Go of True Belief

I expected the Pryns to be fundamentalist fanatics, a repressed couple driven sideways by Elmer Gantry types, two people on a self-appointed mission to punish those who opposed their image of God. I had prepared myself to hear their dogged insistence on the commands of scripture. I did not let myself picture them in any other way. I knew the Pryns, grew up with their kind, and felt it was safer to swap a throat lozenge with a rabid dog than challenge a single one of their beliefs about scripture. I imagined burning crosses and, for some reason, breaking sliding-glass doors. They were middle-class bigots in my mind. To their credit, they didn't disappoint. Standing at the foot of David's bed, I welcomed them to the temporary morgue. I feared for David's corpse.

David denied them the pleasure, the opportunity, any final say. David was now in God's hands, "slippery hands," he shared one night when he doubted God's grace. They could make their claims that he was an apostate, but David never stopped believing in God. He just stopped believing in their idea of God. I knew the Pryns could never point to a time, a moment, when he denied God. To do so, they would have to falsify his faith record. He was baptized, and he was now at heaven's gate, a stone's throw from heaven's outer room. He had walked his desert, not into oblivion as they would have liked, but as a time of thirst and discovery. Would they be content knowing that, believing that?

"Why are his eyes open," Nora Pryn asked. Those were the first words Nora Pryn ever spoke to me during the time I knew David. I shared that the eyelids' muscles are involuntary, something the nurses taught me when I volunteered as a hospice chaplain.

"I don't like it," she said, observing her son, officially dead to her now, and appearing to want no record or reminder that her son might have seen into her soul. Nora Pryn lacked the imagination to commune with the unseen and now pretended no intimacy with her son. The softness of David's final breath still in the air summoned the room to reverence; she preferred to entertain families in the lobby, connecting her idea of eternity with her amusements. It felt like a breach of hospitality to appeal directly to her unsophistication, but I was now in imminent danger of asking myself if hospitality were the most important thing in the room.

I felt my body starting to tremble, my anger bubbling through selected pores of my skin. David had whispered his life to her in doses, trying to penetrate the shell of her life in which he hoped something would rattle, her spiritual principle tumbling inside her. Having tried messiahhood at least once, she had a way about her, a way of looking through half-closed eyelids as if she were thinking of David but scarcely seeing him. It seemed to me the cruelest of intentions.

That night, in her dark, she became her shadow, exhibiting a certain predisposition of looking at life as a personal offense. Her being there that night had the character of grim and disturbing evidence presented in court. She looked down on her son, reminding those of us who tip-toed around the periphery of his bed that he was not her son but only a disagreeable incident of thought. I asked myself if the biblical epithet of wickedness could be applied at this moment. Perhaps it is not wicked to swear falsely, but her conception of gain proved unprofitable to me. She seemed too severe, too unrelenting, and I turned my back to her with deep contempt, which prompted me to utter a decent imprecation. I felt the bitterness that I was trying so hard to swallow rise in my throat. Some disappointments last as long as life, and she possessed more traditions than I even supposed.

She stood against a bare wall, her face frozen as a smirk. I don't know how it happens, even when it happens, but grace will finally and completely succumb. Suspicion wins and there is no going back, and there is no reconsideration. The death wish, so ingrained in her, in every polluted pore, made no difference. She had a fiery finish scheduled for every reprobate she knew. Worse, she was looking forward to watching.

She had pushed her son away with no lifeline. To drive away from David when he was seventeen without one last glance, to position the mirror of her heart so effectively until the gait of her son simply blended in with regulars on the street was absurdly cruel. I wondered then, and now, if, while loving her idea of God, she managed to persuade any that she loved anyone else.

Nora Pryn wished no one well; her sympathies limited. To witness the self-destruction of a person who cannot laugh, or chooses not to laugh, or hates the laugher in the next room, became an experience of joyous exuberance for me. Each day since David's death, I ask God to forgive my aroused sadism. I wished Nora Pryn to be old, her face dangerous, the lines of her bigotry deep as caverns. She was anything but that. Her glasses hid what appeared as earlier beauty. At some point, however, she had relinquished her hair to the easiest exception.

She affirmed the triumvirate of bigotry—her son was gay, a former Catholic, and had been a practicing sexual creature. It would be false to say she needed all three for her to dismiss her son. David was first a homosexual, and she quarantined the image of him having sexual relations with another man. His sexual expression was the marker that she could not abide, and she had decided to sacrifice her son to perdition.

To present oneself to God with such a blackness of spirit is to rest too comfortably and easily in God's grace. Surely, such an intentional decision is fraught with the danger of punishment if one believes in such. She and her husband dropped their son off in the far country when he refused reparative therapy. They turned their back on their son and drove away.

Who is the lost one in the story? I confess I have yet to let myself envision Nora Pryn admitting her lostness. I am yet intrigued, wondering what the joy of being found looks like to one who has never considered lostness. I have thought more than once about how she was lost and what precipitated such lostness. How does one find comfort in religion and its demand for faithful choices, even fateful choices?

The Pryns pushed their son to the side of the world, dismissing him as a teenager in order to receive the glad hand of their supporters. The prerequisites for restoration proved too severe for David--unconditional repentance on his part and renunciation of his sexual identity. David made the tragic and painful decision the relationship was no longer worth the effort required.

David died on a Thursday night sedated. The summary of his life inevitably includes that while we encounter and travel for a season with family, in the end, it is alone that we leave this world.

Chapter Eleven

Protecting God

As a general rule, I would say that human beings never behave more badly toward one another than when they believe they are protecting God. Barbara Brown Taylor

The suffering of a single person is rarely calculated as a subject of religion. People choose sides, invest in one person's life to the exclusion of another. And it is the supreme good fortune always to be in a better position for appreciating people than they are for appreciating you.

David lugged a backpack that drooped to the drag of his ass. He shuffled and stumbled in a way that exhibited great physical helplessness. Interestingly, his gait helped to mark his character as that of a humorous victim whose disabilities were part of the joke. His awkwardness became dear to me.

Each Tuesday night, as his body tired, he let others clean and store the leftovers while he stuffed rolls into his backpack.

"Bread for the world, Jesus always said, and I'm still part of the world," he said to Jack. He recoiled at any thought of being a spectacle or object of pity. He was also practical. A roll before taking his morning medication would settle his stomach.

"You say that every week, David. Take the rolls. We want you to take the rolls. You don't have to justify anything," Jack shot back.

"I will enjoy the bread," he shared. "I eat them with peanut butter and cheese. So good. And as I eat, I know that someone else would enjoy them, too. I wash the bread down with a splash of guilt."

"It's a damn roll, David. Get over it," Jack said.

"There are actually seventeen rolls if we are counting," David said. "And I would have taken more if we had any more. I think I need help."

"You need to go home David," Jack said.

I walked with him out the back door of the church. I stood in the driveway and watched him manage his walk to his apartment without significant problems. The number of steps to his third-floor apartment was an obstacle. Even the fifteen exterior steps to get to the front door proved daunting. He shared that he played mind games at each landing, resting against the ledge, catching his breath between drags on his cigarette and, he said, "thinking bigger thoughts."

"I find I'm quite the poet when I inhale," he said one afternoon when he allowed me to walk him home. "Look at the roots of that big elm in the yard. They look like Grandma Pryn's bunions, sore and thirsty."

In those moments of exertion, which grew increasingly more difficult for David during the Spring of 2009, he found a way to make the stairs his communion. On one challenging climb, he started coughing. In his journal, he wrote, "nothing came out. A guy with his girlfriend walked by and asked, 'are you going to live?' He meant no offense, explaining that they had been asked that a few times, too. I was not offended, but the thought of mortality crept in again. Relentless. No matter how hard I've tried to keep it in another place. If he only knew the implication of such a question."

Writing in his journal became sporadic work. Sometimes no more than a few sentences, very often sentimental and overly sweet, what he acknowledged as "just sweet love, feelings not worthy of repeating, but as meaningful to me as the grandest wisdom." I saw them as shadows wanting desperately to blend into a meaningful whole written by someone with a still hand and purposeful imagination.

"Angels" from the church were in and out of his apartment each day, a burden he endured reluctantly. He did not lock his door during the day. His strength waned with each passing day. The side effects of his medicine left him wobbly as an itinerant drunk, and most days he vomited. He preferred to be alone and to welcome guests when he felt like receiving company.

David took great pleasure in contending against those of us hand-picked to do his will, friends willing to march for him, even justify him. He had one rule for us to follow: Do not touch, rearrange, or consider straightening the piles in his apartment. In the corner of the living area, the gathering pub of mismatched furniture and Catholic icons, David stacked intricate things, bristling things, objects that reminded him about the shape of his life and his impending death: books, discharge papers, and hundreds of empty medicine bottles.

"I am a medicine bottle gardener," he shared one afternoon. "I like to organize. I keep every empty medicine bottle. I arrange them by color and position them in groups."

"They look like a rugby scrum," I said. "Each grouping seems to be positioned to fight for the light."

On numerous occasions, I picked up and read the scraps of paper, notes, prescriptions, appointment cards, scattered like buckshot from a shotgun across the floor. It was a task one performs when one is inattentive or wants to avoid deeper concerns or messy emptiness. David possessed nothing of any value, except the upright air conditioner, which he designated to the neighbor couple next door whose daughter once smiled at him when they climbed the stairs together to their third-floor apartments.

That day, the couple, whose names he forgot regularly, walked behind David, ready to catch him if he stumbled and fell backward. The young mother moved to David's step and pinched the sleeve of his sweater, a simple safety gesture, careful not to overstep David's stated boundaries with a more forceful grip of his arm. They were the elements of preliminary compassion. The couple managed him effectively, their grace soft and gentle while allowing David a modicum of self-dignity.

The father was the kind of man who noticed things, especially the give-and-take of reciprocity. He also weighed the advantages for himself while still willing to let himself fall into grace extended. "Thank you for making room for me in your heart," David shared, coughing up sputum and whatever politeness looked like at that moment.

"Every day, I try and be grateful for something. Today, you two get your names in my journal. You two seem soft enough for each other. I want to give you my air conditioner. It's hot as holy hell up here, and I'm sure it's miserable for you."

"We can't have an air conditioner in our apartment," the father said.

"I know the window sashes are too rotten to hold the weight. I have a floor unit. It works pretty well. You can move it from room to room. I told my pastor to get it to you the day I die. If not, someone from my family will take it. If you find it outside your door, you know I'm dead. No one else will let you know."

"You think it's soon," the mother said, shifting her grip to his elbow with the sleight of hand of a magician.

"I've been hoping for July," David sputtered. "It's a good month to die. Don't ask me why, but I don't want to see another Fall. October is too beautiful for me."

Back and forth they navigated the steps as a heavy-handed quartet, wobbling on one step, then the next. The father prodded David forward, holding his baby in one hard and gripping the other around David's belt, now much too big for his skeleton frame. "At this rate, you might not make it up the stairs," he said.

He was the sort of person who never memorized emotions, reacting deftly to his place among those less fortunate. He thought to himself that there was nothing he had wanted very much to do that day. He might as well embrace a field of kindness.

"He thinks he can be an electrician," the mother shared. "Everything takes twice as long to complete though. Eventually, you have to leave the area to get the classes. He fights the drip, drip, drip of doubt. Snuffs out every dream, but I won't let him quit."

"My favorite emotion," David answered, "comedy amid chaos. Calloused with just a whiff of humor." The father sensed their compassion had a price: the time involved, the inconvenience of genuine compassion and kindness. David's invitation had been brief. "Come, to Hot Meals," he said, handing the mother a loaf of day-old bread. "What's it going to hurt? It's a meal." The father knew, however, the time it takes for one's reputation to be sullied, lumped into a gathered pool of amorphous faces, known simply as Hot Meals guests, was short.

"We have enough food," he said.

"Why are you two here," David asked. "It's a subsidized building. Most people who live here have been around awhile. No one leaves. It's too hard to find a place that will take people on welfare."

"My dad knows the owner," the father said."

"So, I'm living next door to a man with connections," David smiled.

"I guess so," the father answered. "We are trapped for a while, what with the baby and all. I hope it's not forever. I feel stuck."

"Get unstuck," David said.

I stood with friends, women and men as dear to me as distant cousins. They represented the bawdy side of my extended family; the misfits banished to the picnic table nearest the outdoor toilet at our family reunion. These friends, squatters on a promised land they would never own in Seneca, understood how inviting is the pull of smaller tribes. They rented enough emotional space to cause a stir, chopping at the fences erected and rebuilt by the complicit religionists. These friends blew in and out of faith almost daily, exhibiting both a ferocity of spirit for David, as well as a realism that revealed the ugliness of our collective hearts. Life seems poorer when I think of how much I miss them—people like Ruth.

Ruth Nesbit, dead these past four years, lived her last years as a perpetual cancer patient. She encouraged me to write about David and the church angels. We regularly talked about David, she of the opinion that while my time with him was short, those last months together exemplified the fruit planted in his soul years earlier.

"How would you start?" she asked.

"Pissed off, I guess."

"Yeah, can't write about David without including Peter and Nora."

"I was thinking about them the other day. These years since David died and Peter and Nora still living," I said.

"I never see them," Ruth said. "I want to imagine them miserable, but you know how I like to hold a grudge."

"Me, too. I wonder if I can write David's story differently?"

I served as Ruth's executor, even after I left Seneca—a promise I intended to keep with the permission of the new minister at Covenant. Her diagnosis allowed her ample time to write her specific provisions about her final plans. She possessed very little but cherished the things that served as pointers to her beliefs and memories: classic fiction, Thich Nat Hhan, Mary Oliver poetry, and eclectic art collected throughout her journey as a "roadie" journalist.

When I visited Seneca, we sat on her porch which doubled as a cat sanctuary. We talked, and we cried.

"I love you," I said, during a pause, giving our breaking hearts time to return to the proper rhythm.

"You allowed me the freedom to like God in doses. I'm grateful. I love you, too. But remember our deal," she said piercing any pretension.

"You won't let me forget. You remind me each time we talk," I said.

"It's all in the folder I gave you. And everything is paid for."

"I know. No service. Just a party with friends."

"Certain friends," she corrected. "They know who they are. My cousin has the list. She will let people know the time and place. Laugh and cry. You can say something, I guess, but don't make it all about God."

I kissed her goodbye and sidestepped the hospice equipment. As I reached the door, she smiled and said, "You still haven't shown me what you've written about David." Those were the last words she shared with me.

As David's church angels, we affirmed and inaugurated him as our faith totem, the symbol of what at times felt like manufactured fidelity. His aura became our devotion, the object of what we presumed was his innate nobility. We naively assumed our tin man's strength before the first application of oil. We were his blank pages, successfully kept empty, possessing only a tiny fraction of guile and three or four small exquisite instincts: for knowing a friend, for avoiding a mistake, for taking care of each other, and, finally, for knowing when and where, and for whom to cling.

"David is so damn tiring," William shared one evening after leaving David's apartment. A few of us gathered on the stoop for debriefing, careful to avoid the faults in the concrete.

"Evie is with him now. She's doing Raike. I'm done," William continued. "It never seems to be enough for him. We aren't going to save his idea of family. Why are we doing all of this? It takes a schedule of people to meet just his basic needs now. I'll go ahead and put it out there. It's shitty, I know, but how far does our compassion extend? Would we be here tonight if David wasn't gay? Look at all the people served on Tuesday at Hot Meals. I would bet that each person around those tables is carrying physical and emotional pain. Maybe more than David."

"It's a common pain," Camille interrupted.

There were times when Camille, whose life philosophy was more open sea than a risky channel, dropped a remark that at first hearing sounded false. "It's ordinary. It's doesn't smell like injustice, other than being poor is damn hard. Their pain? We know it. We've seen it a thousand times. At least David has the good fortune of dying differently."

"He's figured us out," I shared. "His being gay plays well with our mission statement. He feeds us enough information about his life, his parents, to keep us pissed. He's a victim and just as powerful as an oppressor."

"Cynical?" Lara said.

"A little," I snapped.

"What is it that we want? It will never end, his dependency on us. How do we pull back the lifeline we've extended?" Camille continued. "It's tiresome that we can't tell him he is a conceited ass because he has AIDS. There are times when his disease seems the best part of him; it gives him privileges no one else gets."

"I get that he doesn't know who to trust, that maybe we are those people," William interrupted. "I'm sure he finds some comfort that we aren't leaving, whatever security looks like to him. I know he wants to trust God, but he's still trying to earn points. But we are doing most of the work."

"I have some ugly thoughts running through my head at times," Camille shared. "If he is so desperately ill, there's only one way to prove it, but he doesn't go there. The physical part, yes, but not everything," she said. "He's more like us than we realize. He wants to be remembered, if not fondly, then his memory tolerated, enough to avoid a campaign of an angry family raising money for a gravestone etched with a summary statement of his life written by his mother."

I loved my friends, but they got tired. I got tired. Preparing answers was never our strong suit. We rarely got further than thinking afterward of clever things we could have said instead. We relied on each other as best we could. Compassion demanded energy to keep it from leaking into resentment or feeling put upon. It required a community where the ebb and flow of emotional fatigue was managed as a group to help keep compassion from being polluted.

I confess I co-opted their faith. I was a member of the gathered herd, fifteen or so cattle mucking up our thousand hills, overseeing our pasture of injustice, and grazing on the first secret of sustained compassion—righteous anger.

We blamed David's parents for the exclusion they modeled, their insistence on foisting their exactness and absolutes, and how they inflicted spiritual violence toward their son. Separating from him because of his sexual orientation was not just narrowness. It was wrong. Nora and Martin Pryn fueled our ministry to David, granting us the needed energy to come to David in our way.

Our culprits had been identified, with all their aliases. We chastised them daily in the corner of David's galley kitchen where the grit of his residual pain, his dismissal, his layered resentment, stained our hearts as effectively as the mold staining the bead of caulking that outlined the counter. It was there, surrounded by milky Tupperware, warped from the heat of too many sunny days, that we memorialized gossip's effectiveness. We built our case against his parents through whispers and asides. We surprised even ourselves as to the depth and degree of our righteousness.

We spoke in hushed tones, reviewing our marching orders to combat David's enemies. We developed our sign language, noting that few people have the guts to be an asshole with a megaphone. The condescension was aromatic, as heavy in the air as a moor fog.

There was energy around the table, the emotional passion of a youth sports team before taking the field. We basked in our pleasurable superiority; we affirmed our circle with winks and nods and the rolling of eyes. Our goal was to bask in the afterglow that we were right. We were in need of a cigarette for an appropriate spiritual orgasm.

We spoke the same language, coded to the best faith principles we could write, and prejudiced toward people in the worst ways. It has been said that to read in the service of any ideology is not to read at all, and to believe only to have one's idea of God affirmed is not to believe at all. Some would say we were in trouble.

David repeatedly victimized while in the city. He described his time as my "didn't give a shit period." In the city, he grew indifferent to a possible new chapter, to reasonable possibilities. The souls he manipulated and controlled consumed his life for much of the next decade.

Lostness was our controlling metaphor. Was David lost among friends? Was it enough to be lost together, people who rested and found some measure of comfort in "foundness" because they were accepted? Was David only lost peripherally, lost to lust, and lost to his passion for sex? Is lostness the inability to cogently fashion a belief system beyond oneself?

David's lostness presented as dangerous paths. There was the threat of disease and his cavalier sexual appetite. Still, as I consider his life in its entirety, there existed a spark in his lostness. It surfaced occasionally but was often beaten down by those who wanted to determine the intensity of the flame. He spent the last years of his life blowing on embers whose sole purpose was to blaze. I sense eternity is filled with people lost in life and death, wandering spirits looking for any place to feel safe. David lived out his life as a nomad. He sojourned in life and faith; he never found the safety of permanent lodging.

Chapter Twelve

Purging Faith's Destructiveness

Vladimir: "Do you remember the Gospel?" Estragon: "I remember the maps of the Holy Land. Colored they were. Very pretty....that's where we'll go I used to say, that's where we'll go for our honeymoon."
Samuel Beckett, <u>Waiting for Godot</u>

No writer can purge time of its destructiveness. David struggled mightily to divest himself of old acquaintances still exerting far-reaching influence. There is no erasing of memory, which, while destructive, also includes blessings of the grandest proportions.

"There are people before you that I love," David said. "I can't look back for too long, but I want to. I want to see how far I've come. I'm here because of a few people. They were not perfect, but they were friends who hurt and healed me in ways more normal. A few of them kept God safe from me and for me. When I think of them, I'm not afraid. I fear the people hiding in the dark now, prepared to strike, plotting to harm me. I'm afraid of the hundred small frights; I'm scared of what's going to happen next. There is always a next. I don't know what is waiting for me. I know there is nothing deliberate. I don't imagine Dad waking to how he can upset David today. It's just the story that is in the air, floating above every conversation they have with each other and with the only friends they have."

David's life, largely an ellipsis with too much omitted, was ripe for gossip. He could never muffle the din of the ideological jamborees sponsored by those he would not let himself imagine loving him again. They modeled separation, exclusion, and power, carried out irresponsibly and maliciously. And they were cowards, falling back on God's will when confronted with their theological shenanigans.

David lived with innumerable health problems. Their accompanying side effects quickly bored even his cherished friends, not that we were uncaring, but his physical deterioration was a given. AIDS ravaged his body incrementally, diabolically, and demanding his life. His headaches, the result of lesions on his brain, were relentless, present in most moments of his day, keeping him from restful sleep at night and pounding his thoughts and emotions into submission during the day.

"I have thoughts at night, good thoughts, but I can't play them out. They won't stay," he shared three weeks before his death. "I had a nice thought about Pam the other night, but that's all it was, a nice thought. Somewhere between she is a soft soul, smart and reasoned, I had to let her go. I wanted to list all the things I like about her. Maybe I did, but I can't remember. The throbbing in my head beats everything good back. And I return to the pain. And with the pain is darkness. And the darkness, you know the darkness. It's a bit presumptuous that the darkness keeps coming back when never invited. I want to go to sleep for no other reason but to die. But that's not the way this is going to play out. The only way I'm going to die is to let the lesions on my brain feast until satisfied. I pray I am drugged up that I won't care."

His apartment resembled a drive-through pharmacy, bottles of pills stationed like soldiers, neatly arranged in every room, ready for pick up when he found the energy to move from his bed. David scribbled on the back of an expired prescription, "I can't free myself from my ruptured memory." I found it while rummaging through his apartment looking for headphones that he said were on the nightstand beside his bed, "but I can't remember shit right now," he said over the phone from his hospital room.

David issued me a key to his apartment, a trust I never felt comfortable holding or accepting. I do possess a natural shrinking from moving curtains and looking into unlighted corners, however. His apartment looked like the apartment of any aging maiden aunt, upholstered in dangerous green. I sat on his couch. There were too many lamps and mismatched shades for my taste in the room. It served as his sanctuary of authorized love, littered with his personal clues that revealed the intensity of his secured guilt. Pasted on his bathroom mirror were two sticky notes with Mary and Daniel's names, his sister and brother, the collateral damage of his life, and fight, and flight. Beneath the names were reminders of the apologies he intended to write, scraps of images that, if developed, would serve as the conflicted poetry of his life. His collection of notes and scraps confirmed why his sensible idea of reconciliation would never be realized. It was always a thing to believe in, not to see, a matter of faith, not of experience. They were pieces, fragments, spiritual meanderings in each of the four rooms. I wanted to believe they were spiritual gems. They were all he had, and there was no more significant reason for their being carefully guarded.

I sensed a perceptible hush in his apartment, feeling something of importance was present without offering it a name. David possessed few things, but there was a softness to what he did hold that gave him joy. His notes, precious and sacred, revealed the organization of his heart and how his thoughts worked his will. He determined the pace of any revelation. He was infuriatingly cautious, preferring to tease his feelings easy, as matter of fact, and finding great comfort and inspiration while listening to Cher.

"Have you ever considered there are moments in life when even Cher has nothing to say to us, that turning back time is not even healthy?" I asked while choking back sarcasm as we drove to his doctor's appointment in the city. "Blasphemy," he countered. "I will only admit they are our worst moments."

"It won't go away, the spiritual ambivalence. At night I wrestle with angels and demons. And the demons often win. They find their place in my fear. They call to me, pastor. They screech like sirens, mesmerizing, relentless, and, strangely, comforting. I know I am damaged beyond repair, and I seem to be on the same page with Satan's thugs. I sleep with the nightmare. You'd think I could dream happier dreams, but when you are dying, you can't relax with anything good. You can only project. I don't let myself dream a lot about an afterlife, and I can't seem to shake separation from God and the possible consequences. Go figure."

His first faith story was unable to protect him from his demons. There was nothing to preserve his life but a system, began and supported by his family, leaving him naked emotionally and spiritually.

"Then write a new story," I said. I confess my explanation was automatic; it failed precisely to express what I wanted to be pure thoughts. I wanted to take another track. We talked about eliminating assumptions, especially the myth of theological fingerprints and their initial importance, and how David wished to free himself from the relational bonds that once sustained him.

Experience had not quenched his youth; it had merely made him sympathetic and supple. "I never set out to destroy my parents' understanding of God," he said. "I just wanted to be safe. Now, I feel broken, bruised by every stone they throw at my heart."

"You asked too much," I said. "Your parents have to give up too much of who they want to be. If they let go, they let go of God. God is only viable as long as their cultural and spiritual framework lasts."

We talked around the idea of developing a new language of faith, one that might serve us both as our finest endowment, the inwardness of our past married to the harshness of the present moment. We agreed that if firmly planted in it, we could bring the future to the here and now and possibly make a few plans. We first had shared our spiritual and theological trauma and, if examined truthfully, we might move in the direction of more empathetic interpretations.

David's story revealed the glaring limitations to any consideration of the power of suffering. His suffering was self-inflicted at many points, as was mine. There was nothing new in our quest: trying to reconcile God's nature with suffering experienced in life, inflicted by others, and the temptation to settle for a disabling theology. And then there was the issue of believing God brings about suffering to test faith. What does this say about God and God's judgment on the people who hold such views? There were times we excluded God from our conversation.

"The passages from Leviticus negate my life. But more, they indicate my worth is non-existent. The passage wants me dead," he said, living out the intersection of such pronouncements which, until he came out as gay, were rarely mentioned except to point to the controlling sins that were unforgivable.

"I wear the badge of being a relativist gladly," I said. "I think most people are. I build my theology around my view of God, through a different lens, my lens. It's a spiritual overcoming. There is no victory in my suffering, your suffering, as a victory that leads to something better."

Theology is only investigated in darkness, in the lost points of life. We look for the dawn, but life does not quickly rise from the heap of ashes we know only as sunsets. How deadly is the time between Good Friday and Easter? Suffering does not come through willful disobedience to God; instead, it is an inherent part of human existence. Theology has failed to help people imagine God in a less abrasive way. We assume that in each suffering moment are later consequences, none more damning than God's loving gaze upon us is intentionally muted. Faith flickers, and yet it asks that I watch the night sky and determine my place in God's cosmological playground, that I consider giddiness when confronted with the hint of mystery, that space where final questions, even the first questions, become the only questions. There is only rule: what is hopeful and life-giving, and what is death embracing.

Imprisoned by the Bible, the Pryns sought something to worship beyond dispute. How comfortably they moved to self-deification, becoming minor idols strolling as wobbly toward God as a drunk leaving a local bar. Behind every worshipper lurks Narcissus. In their computation of holiness, the Pryns gave little time for mystery and too much time protecting the Bible.

They contained God in the Ark, God's power as confining as Noah's stalls. They conveniently forgot the manna that daily descended on the Hebrews in the wilderness could not be hoarded from one day to the next without it spoiling. The same is true of faith: it cannot be accumulated. No church, no creed, can save it and it not degenerate. Self-deification robs us of our humanity. David reluctantly served as a sacrifice to his parents' pretentions of deity.

David's life with his parents forced our church to consider the degradation of religious expressions carelessly affirmed and meant to incarnate faith. How easily faith can terminate into superstitious conformism.

"God feels like an accessory," David shared, "a nice broach to complement our religious blouses."

"God is our great failure," I said. "God is too often born out of our necessity. We improvise. I think that's okay as long as we continue to improvise. We freeze God, codify God. Dogmas always betray faith whenever indelible ink is involved. Some of our gods must die, the gods of our own making. We only formulate concepts of God. They are never identical with God. There is always an inadequacy. We invented religion, and we gave ample space for those to invent the God that dies. It is the failure of Christians that we don't consider taking the sword to our ideas about God. My favorite Kafka quote is "Christianity is the thorn bush in the road that must be set ablaze if we want it to go further."

"Christianity has never been tried," David said. "It's too hard; it's ideals too difficult and demanding."

"Maybe it's not pure enough or demanding enough," I countered.

"I think faith is easy if God is reduced to the convenient attributes of a blind idol. God and incredible niceties," he said, revealing his love for sarcasm.

Theological illiteracy, or as Job describes it to his careless friends, "The Proverbs of Ashes," is untenable to people unable to consider God apart from what they first learned and took into their hearts. Job's friends were unwilling or unable to accept responsibility to embark on a journey that was their own. And they resented Job for trying.

David's parents were spiritual abusers, making David's life as miserable as possible. They wished him stoned but kept missing, symbolizing the aimlessness of self-righteousness. They claimed authority, what they named as faith's mysterious preoccupation. They possessed no legal authority, and what they did to David was certainly not moral. Their cost of spiritual authority was a non-starter for David, too much for him to pay. He stopped trying to justify himself to them. "There is no justification of my first life," he shared, "but I can't imagine a life where there is no excitement for new possibilities. I am just now finding what I wanted to be. Why would I submit to their right to insult or oppress me?"

Chapter Thirteen

Humility Before God is Always an Option

"Love is as august a religion as any." Baudelaire

David and I had been sweetened by association. He possessed more than his share of charm, and his health did not always seem like a limitation. On most occasions, however, his illness served as an emotional advantage; it absolved him of professional emotions and leaving him the luxury of being exclusively personal on his terms.

He listened to us with great attention at first, as if what we said, even how we cared, warranted his attention. He quickly grew tired of our investment in him, however, leaving us feeling he was now only half-thinking and merely accommodating himself to the weight of his pain. He favored short visits, preferring his thoughts to our interruptions. We were left with compassion to spare; we wasted its essence which was worth more to us than to David. Too often, we departed his apartment irritated that we kept silent, never uttering a word to defend our presence.

David had had to consent to be desperately ill, yet he tried desperately to escape being formally sick. We were his daily reminders that he failed. David was bright and prickly; he was disturbingly dying and cared little for new friends and merely tolerated his old ones.

"Are you tired," Lara asked, her anxious eyes and her charming smile as touching as a child's prayer.

"Always," he snorted. "Today, very much so. And I am pissed I continue to wither. I wake up in the morning and death has etched another line. Literally. Look at my face. Cracked like the steps on the porch. God, I know I am on a journey, but it would be nice when I get there if I am invited to dance looking half decent."

"You need to eat something," she said. "You've been living on air and cigarettes." There was no particular reason why Lara should challenge him, but there was a quiet misery about David that irritated her. She had raised delicate kindness to an art; she left no space for the narrow ways of deception that flitted in front of David's life and that he, more than once, found enjoyable.

"I'm not hungry. Before you leave, however, set aside another bowlful of air. I'll eat it later when I smoke," he said dismissively.

"You possess the fine quality of being an ass," she shot back."

He looked puzzled; his gaze as uncomfortable as his bed. He intentionally hesitated to take part in any continuing conversation with her for the longest and most frustrating of time. Lara said nothing. When people were embarrassed, she usually felt sorry for them, but she was also determined not to help David utter a word that would not honor her presence in the room.

"I'm not trying to destroy anyone but myself," he said, finally, repositioning toward her and his wall. "I'm not envious. I wouldn't hurt anyone intentionally; I just want to be like them. I'm only hurting me. It's where I am. I know the consequences," he said.

"You pick and choose when you want to feel sorry for yourself," she said with a measured calm that, if half-listening, one misses the initial sting of the barb until later and when the timeliness of a proper rebuttal has passed. "And you do hurt people. You get some leeway from me, others, but you have our hearts, and you stomp on them with regularity."

"So, I am supposed to die and make you feel better at the same time," he countered. "Forgive me if I don't take up the challenge. And if we are being honest, you have an annoying habit of pissing me off. I don't have the strength to fly where you want me to fly. How's that? he said, his voice rising in anger. "I don't have the time to ask you if you are enjoying the view. I prefer walking with my memories instead of flying. They are mine, and I will invite whomever I want to walk with me. The terrain is all mine, created by me from all that has happened. I know every scrape, prick, and blister. It's mine, but I am too tired to walk alone anymore. I wake up each morning hoping the next rise is the last one. I pray it is. You want me not to look back, but that's what dying is, Lara, looking back, wishing it might be different. You want me to feel something I can't feel; I don't have the energy to keep you entertained. I try on one emotion each day, and people will have to decide if they want to watch me change. Last night, I thought about peace and about how far I've come. That should put you and the crew at ease, don't you think?"

David paused just long enough to remind Lara why she loved him. "I do envy those who soar above it all, above their pain, their destination always within their mind's possibility. It hasn't been that way for me. I want you to understand, but I can't lead you along."

"I just think it would be nice if you could say thank you without grinding your teeth," she said, smiling, forgetting hurtful words as easy and regularly as she forgot her glasses.

David spent much of his life seeking freedom from the theological prison that fiercely occupied his heart and mind. He found release in fragments, but he could not escape forever the temptation to return to his earlier and more comfortable cell. When faith comes up against pain and abandonment, sometimes the chasm created appears too wide.

"The past is not in the past, Lara," David continued. "There is no pretending the wounds aren't there, never hit the mark. The scars are mine, all mine. I am grateful, Lara, that you are here, this day."

David wrestled with multiple assumptions, particularly the ones trying to win the last days of his faith journey. He read the Psalms regularly for peace and hints of assurance.

"There is wisdom and foolishness on every page," he shared. "And then I read the Gospels and the time Jesus offers a concrete example of building my life following the plans of wise and foolish builders. 'The fear of the Lord is the beginning of wisdom,' he continued, "that who or what we fear and follow becomes our religion. I've lived my life as a theological bee, flitting from one flower to the next, believing, hoping, the nearest bright rose will serve as my next faith loophole."

Assumptions damage and we don't realize the extent of the damage until we face our dying. Some we carry from childhood: overachieve to be accepted; sickness equals weakness; another person will make us content. The deadliest of assumptions are those we make about God. We follow the old agreement of fear, signed by those who never meant us harm. People assume specific interpretations of God. That is the beauty of diverse theological thought, but the interpretation is always an experience and not a direct line to God. And assumptions turn deadly when whole groups agree on unquestioned assumptions. God must be appeased. Someone has to pay, and someone has to suffer for God to be happy, to keep God happy. Such beliefs and their accompanying power and persistence are life-defeating. They keep us imprisoned in the past. The past is not insignificant, but to assume what happened in the past will determine what will happen in the future is an intolerable way to live. When we are surprised by life as it unfolds, forgetting past mistakes or holding others to past mistakes, we open ourselves to possibility. We are rich in faith when we are able to meet the requirements of our imagination. If I ask, is homosexuality condemned in scripture, my response is yes and no. However, if I ask how my understanding of God has changed because I developed a relationship with a gay man, then I am on my way. Something has to give. I must let go of either my understanding of scripture as infallible, or my heart's tug that I need to assign myself to a human being who has a story.

Scripture never states that it must be read literally; it does encourage reading it, however. Our language is so inadequate as we presumptuously try to speak for God. I blame Martin Luther. When he opposed the teaching of the Catholic hierarchy, he needed a superior authority. He needed the Bible. There is a maniacal obsession with the Bible, and yet it cannot answer every question, clarify certain statements, arbitrate disagreements, or deal with new developments. For those who need certainty, they will eventually find it in the texts. I do wonder if it is worth the effort.

David's first church owed its origin to social and cultural differences that set them apart and away from any who might disagree with their moral premise. They never challenged their animosities, and they never considered that God could become irrelevant. They missed how easily love becomes a brute force without taming. They suppressed love as a spiritual gift mediated through interactions with flawed human beings. Love played out as a drip, quenching no one except those closest to the spigot.

David loved them despite their betrayal. Curiously, I wanted them to love David. I watched him sift through the rubble of his life, spending far too many hours scratching for crumbs, a fragment of affirmation extended by his adversaries. He rethought his assumptions, primarily his belief that an interpretation was not reality. It is an iconoclasm. When assumptions proved untrue or not applicable, when, having failed as an interpretive lens by which he viewed God, he rested on new assumptions that served his revised intentions. Assumptions do not give up the ghost easily, however.

David's story began with assumptions about God and God's story as presented in scripture.

"There always seems to be more than one story in every story," he said. "There is always a subplot. Every story has minor characters who illuminate the primary meaning of the story. I'm a minor character; I am not the protagonist. I am the protagonist's friend."

"I think that's true," I said. "When I think of Abraham, I wonder about his relationship with Sarah after she learned what Abraham had set out to do, sacrificing their son, Isaac. Did Sarah run from that kind of religion, born out of fears, pleas, and entreaties, all the while trying to get a handle on God's inexorable insistence? How did she live with God who forced believers to do something horrible to please God? I wonder how she managed the dark side of religion."

When the idols we have constructed crumble, when suffering is at ease dancing around our golden calves, our place in the story changes. Suffering is no longer a fierce idol projecting God's condemnation. Faith for those suffering is not judgment; it becomes better news. The person is free from guilt, from shame, and the church can become more than the site of perpetual spiritual violence.

Theological power finds expression in the community of faith: reflecting the saving love of God, enabling people to perceive light in the darkness, even becoming the light, and reacquiring hope in despair. But too much of the time our language about God is practically impotent; our inability to capture any idea of God beyond our reality.

Faith traditions, beleaguered from the wars of setting things in the right places and time, forget the ultimate importance of the call from the weeds of the world, women and men impervious to grace sounds and deaf to the words left on the hearts of those who possess opposing emotions.

I grew up a Southern Baptist. Its claim to fame, beyond is its great mission work of sharing the good news of a loving God, is scripture is first, primary, before God, even before any thought of God. It serves as the ultimate test of faith before any mention of God. They deify the Bible because the humanness of each textual story is too fraught with possible misinterpretations. They appear unaware that the resulting aftermath is littered with bodies of people spiritually blown to pieces.

There are tears in every story, tears shed by those at the mercy of a charismatic preacher's interpretation. David, fragile in ways he never wanted to name, defied suffering only as he found a way not to give in to it or move toward it and its accusations during the day. The power to remain human in the face of what appeared to him as inhumanity was enough for most of his days. He believed God would hold his suffering across the ages until there would be an accurate accounting across time.

Certainty cannot be an object of veneration, a fierce idol supporting anything like God's condemnation. Faith grows from stories. David's story played out as the story of human nature, the prospect of evil lurking behind the softest expression of grace. I felt called into his story. I responded to it because as I would learn the dead have stories to tell through their lifeless bodies and tightly closed lips.

Despite Kubler-Ross's assessment, David never approached conventional calm as he advanced toward death. Pale and bruised, but still responsive most days, his face became indistinguishable from the cotton sheets on his bed. His thin whiskers languished upon his lean cheeks, and the curve of his nose defined itself more sharply as his weight fluctuated. His physical deterioration, however, kept him strangely alert to his spirit which had not taken the same beating.

There is an audacity in any theological undertaking or reflection. It is wholly ludicrous to consider for more than a minute that we can speak about God intelligently. Anything more is blasphemy. There is a proper passiveness to be learned in suffering, for example. Its meaning is found in how we receive what comes our way. To work to become theologically literate, beyond the siren call of daily rationalizations, or searching for loopholes that fit our cultural and social constructs, or giving into destructive patterns, means, at least, our perceived knowledge of God is always transitory and ever moving. It leads us to undesired destinations we would rather avoid. And those places, we can rage against them if we want, pour out lament if we need to, or we can bear them with the Christ. That, too, is faithfulness; passive, passionate and meaningful. I wished that for David.

"What you do each Sunday drives me crazy," he said. "I couldn't do it, and it bothers me that you want to do it."

"The sermon?" I asked. "Why is my preaching a problem?"

"I don't want to talk about God all the time, and I certainly don't want to let anyone else in on our conversation. We are listening in, pastor, eavesdropping on your heart. It should be yours and yours alone. You don't offer any resolutions; you leave us with a lump in our throats and expect us to deal with it."

"I don't know any other way to do it, but you're right my sermons are conversation starters. I've never liked the word "preacher. Too much bad history in the word. There's a reason people shout, 'don't preach to me.' Too many platitudes. My faith doesn't respond well to certainty."

"There must be something else you could have done with your life," he said, "a safer, more productive line of work."

"I've thought about that. I know myself a little. I know I'm afraid of math. I enjoy science but not the rigors of experimentation. I love the majesty of science more than the constructs. I like to think about the universe and how it has played out. It's theological, looking for loopholes and imagining how God fits or doesn't. I'm not sure that pays well, however. I'm a fair writer. I can preach a little. Most days, I feel I am where I am supposed to be."

"Your best gift, pastor, is also your most annoying gift. You listen with your heart. Most people listen for a code, a word or phrase, that solves the riddle of what they can do. You look for ways to enter their story."

"Well, just be careful of false prophets," I said. "Avoid them at all costs. I'd say they are out for your money, but you don't have any money. David, as you look at your life now, and if I were to ask you to decide between trust or mistrust as your beginning assumption about God, which would you choose? Perhaps you have already chosen, but is there one thing that has become a non-essential that you can't let slide without letting slide your identity as God's child?"

"People take life apart and put it together the way they want, in ways that do not work for them, and especially for no one else. My earliest impressions of God were tinged with negativism. I thought, "thy will be done" meant I was asking for suffering; to obey God was to say goodbye to joy and pleasure. I don't feel that way now."

Chapter Fourteen

Story is More Important Than Theology

Live your questions now, and perhaps without knowing it, you will live along some distant day into your answers. Ranier Maria Rilke

Theology does not make us see, but a story does. And poor theology makes us blind to people. Theology shapes things in a certain way. There is a normative rule of the academy to follow: God's poetry translated into prose. There is nothing wrong with the exercise; it is not sinful. I sense it may be tacky, however, as inappropriate as a smoker lighting a cigarette from the altar candles after a wedding or a guest wearing a gray suit to a gala. Indeed, the theology of the establishment cannot be made alive by developing another set of propositions and doctrinal assertions.

David fell into a deep depression in the last months of his life. We spoke in dribs and drabs about what he felt was essential, but he didn't have the energy to believe it true anymore. Discovering his unrealized potential had served as a lightning point for most of the last three years, but now he grieved that he had yet to figure out how to nourish his potential enough to bring it forth to the world.

"Bringing out what you have learned may be more difficult than going deep into your soul in the first place," I said. "You've sought something, found it even, but there is always the chance that nobody will care or pay attention. I guess you have to decide if you want to be indebted to the opinions of others."

"I think I do," he said. "I would like to think my search has been worth writing down and remembered around whatever campfire people who do that sort of thing do around a campfire."

David's honesty could be off-putting, harsh and unfair, but there was something trustworthy about his journey. He articulated his story well, but it was never the sum of the truth to which his story pointed. His story held theological seeds within itself and included his best efforts to save himself from the beasts that surrounded his spirit. It became a receptacle for healing in its ability to rectify the blandness of his poor dreams. And, admittedly, his story was also an insult to those who wielded power over him. He lived in paralyzing fear of who would control his narrative.

Joseph Campbell wrote there are only two kinds of stories in the world: The hero who takes a journey and the strangers who come to town. Our stories are rooted in human experience, and while we may not be heroes, we are on a journey. We connect with characters, life affirming or death embracing characters and their multiple plot incarnations along the way. Explaining to someone that strict legalism related to faith is dead means virtually nothing to someone who lost their life to alcoholism and gotten it back. To this person, there is a clear and pronounced narrative that resonates: God is the hero. Conversely, telling someone whose only image of God is negative, judgmental, and retributive that there are other interpretations of God means little to someone whose mind has generalized God as a villain, an interloper who has no right to make any demands.

I have endured ten-plus years of disappointment, thinking that others positioned themselves in David's life forcefully enough to win his story. These days, I still marvel at how he could push past their rejection of his life. His faith journey was never about winning, at least not on the first attempt. I am grateful he didn't risk the adventure alone, that he included me to walk with him, and that I began to understand the labyrinth outside my door during our time together. We followed a thread that we hoped was God. Where we thought to find only fault lines, we found God; when we thought we might find a reason to harm, we found the strength to release its potency into the abyss; where we thought we would be alone, we found ourselves walking with dear friends, even the whole world; where we thought the journey was outward, we found enough sustenance to rest in God, not asking God for anything but presence.

David ventured forth from a familiar world into strange and threatening places. At the boundary of the familiar and unexplored resides what Joseph Campbell names as the "threshold guardian." It represents one's shadow, the portion of oneself rejected over time. David begrudgingly accepted his rejected personality, while at the same time gaining access to an inner strength which proved invaluable even as it played out too slowly for his liking.

"I don't know God as an idea," David shared. "I only know God as presence."

"Well, if it's comforting, there were probably three hundred books published last year dealing with God as an idea," I said, "and not one of them sold very well."

"Then any idea of God can't be God completely, right?" he pressed.

"Definitions seem to get me in trouble. There is a language that ministers learn early, or they won't survive in some churches. You dance around what you really believe, what you hope to share. You try to find a way to stay true to what you believe without undermining people's faith. It's a tightrope we walk. I almost got fired when I said I didn't think Jesus' crucifixion was the will of God. The more I tried to explain what I meant, the deeper I got. They had a deacon's meeting after. They didn't vote to remove me, but they didn't trust me anymore."

"Church people are pussies," he said.

"Well, some, maybe, but not at Covenant. You've been a part of the adult forum class. That group is thirsty. People found a place where they can share their doubts about some of the doctrines that have troubled them but were afraid to share. They trust they won't be excoriated. You were in the session when Evie shared that she had had an abortion when she was a young woman. And then someone else shared a similar experience. No one said much of anything, but I looked around the room, and all I saw were tears. That's all we had to offer, our weeping, that her pain we just too big and too confusing for only one person's tears. That was one of my best days as a minister. What a trusting place that a woman could offer to us her deepest wound, something she had been carrying around for years. That would never have happened in my first church. They were kind enough, but there were conversations we couldn't have. I wanted them to adopt a new baptism policy, that people did not have to be re-baptized if they wanted to join the church. They massaged the forces and voted it down. They were stuck, and I was too young to help them out. I don't think church members are pussies; they are frightened."

"Like I said. Church people are pussies," David affirmed.

"That opinion is more convenient for you, isn't it? I hate talking to you when you are enjoying being a jerk."

"Probably true. I guess I'm just thirsty. How thirsty must I be to leave my broken cisterns? You spend time thinking about the Nicene Creed?" he asked.

"That's a segue," I said, knowing I was deflecting with poor humor. I knew he was living out his best life and trying to beat back assumptions that he knew could no longer save him or pay off. "Not every week," I said, "but I guess every sermon is some kind of reflection on the creeds, a translation of some principle contained in the creeds." I stated what I thought was appropriate. It was everything but natural.

"I just say the creed. Well, not anymore, but when I was Catholic, I said it every day," David continued.

"Congratulations, you can now say you stand with the majority on something," I said. "Most people don't give a tinker's damn about the creeds, but people used to. They felt like they had to because some people were taking God into places that felt uncomfortable. Some people thought they wanted conformity, even held meetings and argued and hammered out who would win. And the creeds are the written records of who won, what the church would present as orthodox. But there was a large number of people who, while in the minority, kept offering different interpretations of God, especially women. And now there are gay scholars who are writing from their context. How they hear scripture as good news is beyond me."

"Most gay people don't hear it, and they don't go to church. And they certainly don't read scripture," he said. "I have conversations with God; that's all. God knows my story, stories, plural. Jesus comes along for the ride. Can't really say that is theology, though. It's not deep. It won't hold up to Joseph or Elinor or Ann, but it's enough for me."

"I think theology is fluid," I said, "like God washing over the stories of our lives. And thinking about God shouldn't end, even as it seems to have an end. The end becomes a beginning again, creating a beginning out of an end."

David was always more than a single story. He was gay. He was also funny, insightful, and ferocious about certain elements of his story that pushed him beyond his sexual orientation. He certainly didn't fit into a single story. I confess I had in my head when we first met, he could only be gay. I offered only well-meaning pity because I believed he had but one story. I presented as no different from some in the Christian community in Seneca who interpreted his life as an abomination, and that he would eventually get his. I began my story with David assuming he was dying of AIDS, lived in material and spiritual poverty, and was waiting to be saved by kind white progressives. And David's parents, I didn't think they could be anything but strident and exclusive. It was my default position, and it was patronizing and divisive. I felt I could take up the task of summing up their shallow lives.

The one-dimensional story that someone uses to describe us, or flattens our experience, makes things easier for others. The stereotype plops so uncomfortably on our hearts and minds that sometimes breathing is difficult. We inch our way toward God who knows our every thought and our every hope, our every gift and every broken place, every single beautiful thing about us, every remarkable story and even the ones that aren't so remarkable. We are the subject of God, the storyteller, our storyteller.

We wrestle with stories concerning our sexuality, emotional desires, solitude, and thoughts of intimacy. Still, other stories lie in wait to pounce, stories of darkness, real or imagined, stories of feeling unwelcome. We miss scenes of healing because they have never lived up to their billing, and too often they appear conditional. We learn to map our lives according to the signs of the world instead of the stars. Reconciliation looks like what we want it to look like.

On most days, David leaned toward believing he was loved. He felt that early in his life, but for the majority of his youth his parents told him many lies about himself when he announced he was gay. He had to spend too much time unmasking his manipulative and controlling corner of the world when he should have been exploring. One early morning as he dressed for an appointment, he shared, "I know I say it too much but this time I have been hurt. I don't think I can bounce back from this. I think I want to close my eyes and click three times. I want more than anything to wake up in God's home."

"And the drama begins early today, I see," dismissive laughter my go-to response to most of David's drama.

"I know we don't do syrup and sweetness, pastor, but can't you be uncomfortable for a minute. Don't shit on this, please. I got a letter from my mother," he shared.

"Your mother," I said incredulously.

"Yeah, she wrote to tell me that I am the reason Dad has heart problems," he said as he navigated his t-shirt. "I'm the one, the reason, Dad was in the hospital."

"That's a new level even for your mother," I said.

"I thought so," he said. "And I don't want to talk about it." We didn't. We never spoke about it again.

The strength of faith is its manners, how well it eats with suffering. I wished for David a way out; I wanted him to find release in some manageable way that allowed him to retain some measure of integrity. He wished it so, others who drew close to him wished it as well. It would happen, but not in the way we imagined. There would be no restoration, which always seemed the one characteristic of faith that had sustaining power. It melted on the burnt sidewalk of his path as we walked to the car. His effort, always an amazing effort to make peace, had been dismissed finally and completely.

What happens to a person who chooses a different path, but no one, except for a few friends, who, while they are important, are not supremely important, come to see you off but never consider walking with you and enjoying your company. What happens to the soul when family proves inadequate for deeper emotions, content to dig around the surface of one's life? What happens when a letter arrives from your mother blaming you for all that has gone wrong?

"You spoke to me that my life was enough. I assume you mean the final version," David shared. "Why was it not enough when I was at my lowest? Is that God's idea of a joke, that speaking of grace was just a throwaway line, that in the end, I would have to change into some more respectable form."

"Of course, you had to change, not for grace's sake, but for your sake," I said. "You couldn't think of grace while in the city. You spent ten years running from any idea of God. Grace was always there, present to you in capsule form, the medicine that might provide ultimate healing. You first had to find healing by acknowledging your wounds, your self-inflicted wounds. Your life, my life, reside so close to oblivion; the edge is close, the ledge steep and severe, and grace steps in to ask the simple question: Is this all you want? In this great world, all you want out of it is to survey its depths, the hell that is our planet, disease, illness, mistrust, hatred, and indifference. That's all you wanted."

"David, I've pretended my whole life to know something about grace. I've wanted to believe it because I can't bear the legalism of faith. But I want you to know I've kept my secrets secret, secrets only known to a few besides the people I've wounded. Grace is something that has kept me on a path. Did it make me kinder, less judgmental toward others? Maybe. Does it make me a better pastor? I hope so. Can I ever rid my heart of the need to be accepted, affirmed? I am still waiting.

I've been around death; I've seen it play out in every conceivable way. I've seen the aftermath. I've seen families resentful still, even as the body of their loved one is body-bagged for a trip to the funeral home. I've watched families still guarded to any different reading of the deceased. In those moments, when death is at its ugliest, families will pile on additional lies, suspicious of any different interpretation offered regarding the dead person's character."

David's story, while containing literal truth, felt more metaphorically true. To the degree that some got caught up in following the progression of every jot and tittle in his life as a gay man, the rightness and wrongness of his life, they missed his life's power. The more I listened to his heart, however, the more I realized his life revealed a larger truth—the discovery of who we are raises our spiritual consciousness to the mystery we call God. David's life became a field of reference, a guideline to consider beauty.

Why take up a journey that appears at first glance to be perilous, walking the crooked lanes of one's labyrinth and finding oneself among a landscape of figures, any one of whom may swallow us. In matters of faith, my tendency is to avoid fixed stars. For some, there is comfort in their permanence, but, for me, they shine as an incomplete horizon.

David possessed many good qualities, none more sustaining than his innate ability to compartmentalize the ugly thoughts he held toward many, toward those who refused to give him what he most wanted and needed—a safe goodbye.

Chapter Fifteen

Our Justice and God's Justice

I must have justice...And not justice in some remote infinite time and space, but here on earth, and that I should see it myself...And if I am dead by then, let me rise again, for if it will happen without me, it will be too unfair. Surely, I haven't suffered, simply that I, my crimes and my sufferings may manure the soil for future harmony for somebody else. I want to see with my own eyes the hind lie down with the lion and the victim rise up and embrace his murderer. I want to be there when everyone suddenly understands what it has all been. Fyodor Dostoevsky, <u>The Brothers Karamazov</u>

I can't remember a time in which I did not have grown-up concerns about God. I was handed an unhealthy relationship with God early in my life; God either punished me for each misstep or tried to build character by bringing trials into my life. What kind of petty God would sit around and throw a stick for me to fetch, erect an obstacle course for me to navigate, to transform me into some robotic likeness of cruelty? I believed, not because I thought God was wonderful, but out of habit. Despite the years of trying to rid myself of such inanity, I am still afraid of skipping church.

I've thought more than once about extending to Nora Pryn my heart. I still wonder about her childhood. Did she ever feel abandoned, out of control, and insecure? Did she make herself susceptible to those emotions, or did she try and control her world by sheer willpower? Was she praying for God's will to be done, or trying to force God to do her bidding?

I imagined nothing changing her mind. She survived the loss of her son to his sexual orientation because of her fierce beliefs. I suspect she would have withered if she had had to give up her strident theology. There were times I was tempted to break her world apart because of the damage she inflicted on David. I cannot think of him without some level of anger and bitterness I still have toward her. She wounded David in ways colored by the darkest ebony. Even after these years since David's death, I am trying to make sense of her journey. I want to read again the stories she reads because, like great fiction, the stories of scripture reveal truth about people's understanding of suffering, of trials, of hardships. Perhaps this endeavor will help me figure out how to frame my journey, as well as help me understand why I want to keep Nora Pryn in my heart as the saddest of misinformed souls.

I dream of restoration in all its forms, directed to some who have entered and stayed in my life for all these many years. Restoration was never our practice growing up; we forfeited the language of grace. The simplest words which might be profoundly healing remained hidden or tucked away for an appropriate time, leaving me to sleep with the damnable silence of shame. The code in our family was utilitarian; affection was withdrawn to re-establish honor, and the offender was always invisible.

When life returned to a battered normal, it was not the wound, even the infection, that proved so destructive. I returned to the only thing I knew, retreating to whatever and wherever I hoped was safe. I wanted to run toward something more graceful but was unsure and unsettled as to what might heal my spirit; there were times I searched for someone who had no desire to draw out humiliation further or maximize my penance.

At some point, this fright became about me and only me. I didn't possess healing tools. What would my failures feel like if I was offered a safety net, even as I openly acknowledged my missteps and blatant sins? Was it possible to wrap my wrongdoing in a new language? All I knew was our flawed family theology and our voyeuristic obsession with another's failures. They both sustained me only as rebuke. I am often reminded of Brene Brown's words: "Shame cannot survive being spoken, and shame cannot tolerate resurrection."

The way of Jesus is reconciliation; his pleasure is grace, but I was unclear as to how it would take shape. I sensed Jesus had little time for retribution. Throughout his ministry, he chose instead to focus on relationships, on reconciliation. I've spent my life wanting to believe he was offering me freedom from the spiritual paralysis of the only faith I knew or thought I wanted to know.

What could be a finer thing to live with than a high spirit attuned to softness. I spent too much of my life trying to read my book of life, finding nothing of value that might reward me for my inconveniences. I try to read it properly now, seeing my life, despite all the mistakes, as a delightful story of avoidance, my propensity to have a dialogue with myself for much too long and forfeiting the wisdom of friends who ask me to move on.

I re-read a piece I wrote in my journal during David's death watch. "I watched a young man die yesterday. If I had had a choice to attend, I would have declined. I knew the family only superficially. They were the parents of a daughter I married at some distant past. Their son was now dying, and they thought of me, which clearly proves the oddity of most connections.

I watched the hands of the father, in them forgiveness, as he stroked his son's face with a cool cloth, that in some comical way became flesh and bone compassion. Reconciliation and healing drew as close as love would allow. There is a vulgarity when witnessing a person's end, waiting interminably for life to escape from the body finally. Tears dripped from the father's face like the soft but persistent drops of melted ice cream on the fingers of one's heart. I imagined other moments in this young man's life when his father touched his face, maybe wiping his tears. Why would this moment of dying not become the most blessed of chances to extend love? His tender touch toward his dying son possessed an untapped power to rewrite the ending of his heart.

The too-tired for life son and the weary father insisting their goodbye be graceful finding their joint rest together. This young man, determined to resign from life, had yet again tried to take his life. This time he would be successful, though he had been killing himself for years. My mind returned to the story of the prodigal son and how, in the end, whether we consider ourselves the prodigal or the older brother, our call is to learn what we can from the father."

While in the canyon, it is still possible to miss the beauty of the canyon. The scenery from the rim is different from the view while rafting on the river. In the canyon water, the jutting crags and the bends become obstacles to see around. The canyon now becomes something to possess and rule over. I cannot recreate the mood or emotion I might experience from the rim while on the river. From the rim, I make a deep bow to the river and the odd geological shapes and escarpments thrown together in patterns and beauty and possibility; the view is a refutation of the blindness of analyzing too closely how God speaks. It is only with my heart that I can see rightly.

David's horizon, that sadly played out only as the whims of a dying young man, challenged and admonished him with regularity. There were too many times when it presented to him only as waiting for the muddy water of his soul to settle and become clear. How long could he wait, and was it possible to wait beyond this short time span called life? Even reconciliation with partners, the people who loved him unconditionally, who drew near to him without expectations, proved dicey. I suppose he reconciled to the creation, but the satisfaction felt empty because he never reconciled with his parents, even Mary and Daniel, his sister and brother. I still rest with some measure of peace that David's failed effort at reconciliation never betrayed his first understanding of peace. He reconciled to the only thing he could grasp, the memory of what he wished for.

I asked near the end how he would have lived out his life if he had not acquired AIDS, or if some drug, some cocktail, was available to him early that would help him manage his disease and restoring to him whatever life he wanted to pursue. It was easy insensitivity, a terrible instinct that I possessed, so allied to self-defense that it had become habitual. There were certain corners of my heart that were impenetrably black. The shadows in David's life were gathering, and it was as if I had turned off the lights to his soul, every light between us now vague and thin. I dismissed his life for my want of answers.

"Are you asking me how my life would have played out, freed from AIDS, or are you asking me how I would have lived if I wasn't gay?" he said.

"Freed from AIDS. How would you have lived as a gay man without the fear of dying because of AIDS?" I stressed.

"I don't know what you want from me, pastor?" he shared. "It feels like you are trying to wrap my life up in some way that you can manage. There is a question under your question. Do you want to know if I would still have faith, still think of God from time to time?"

"I don't know what I'm asking, David, why I'm even asking. I just can't let go of how you found the strength to consider God. Was it some spark, something you learned, and didn't even know you learned about God early?"

"I don't have an answer. I'm scared when I think I would have been who I was in the city for the rest of my life. There was nothing there to stop me; there was no one to stop me. I can't live that question too long. I know AIDS stopped me. Would I have stopped pissing on my life without the diagnosis? Dear God, I don't know. I don't know," he said, dropping his head in the corner of the quilt folded neatly at the foot of his bed. He sobbed for too long, unable to speak. Finally, he said, "it's too hard of a question. I don't want to think my illness is the only way God could get me to stop, but I can't be sure. I don't know, pastor, I don't know."

"People share with me that they are seeking God, searching for God," I said. "They are on a specific journey to nab what is holy. It feels right when I listen; there should always be movement in any spiritual journey. None of us can say we have fully arrived, however. The danger in any journey is to make us into the hero of the story, that we are the active ones, as if we are playing a spiritual game of hide and seek, that God is hiding from us and we are the ones actively seeking. God is always before us, awaiting us at some distant place."

"You think God was searching for me in the city? All my life, even?"

"I do."

"I didn't think God could find me there? I don't remember putting down any bread crumbs," he continued.

"David, you kept getting up each Sunday and going to church with your parents. You knew how your parents felt; you knew how their church felt about you being gay. Daniel said you use to lead the children at church, but they took that away from you. You kept going back. Why?"

"I needed money. Dad had an envelope for me," he said dismissing any realistic appraisal of grace.

"Maybe," I said. "But I wonder if back then you thought of God differently. Your dad could have dropped off the money at another time and place. I sense your father would have found a way. You were young, but were you deciding differently about God, especially about the God in their stories."

"I hope you are right. I mean about God looking for me. You are giving me too much credit for being wise. I was anything but wise. I think I just needed to dream," he said.

Hope is a renewable vow, daily exercised. Despair is its antithesis; it feels absolute, an immovable emotion, winning most days by default. I sense we descend into it by simply following the wrong god home. It is always possible to turn our ears to other interests. I've spent most of my life asking people to move from fear and exclusion to that of appreciation, empathy, and friendship. I confess I have not always lived as if it were true, but it has always felt right as a beginning assumption.

I feel more at home now with my religious language; it is more than capable of naming for me what it means to be in right relationship with God. I failed to recognize that my antipathy to beliefs and practices I found unenviable created an isolation bubble. My sense of success in the face of other faiths, which may be the most agreeable emotion of the heart, reveals nothing but more isolation and destruction.

Fundamentalism, as expressed by the Pryns, is all too clear. They felt no need to examine other faith traditions except as illustrations of what to avoid and how to prop up their understanding of Christianity. They claimed their anchor, their holy writ, sacred only for the answers it gives rather than the questions it asks.

The myth of theological fingerprints determines which story will win our lives. What are we willing to risk? What do we choose to make dear from our past, the printed paragraphs of necessary salvation? To lose track of the questions about things that matter always, life and death questions about meaning, purpose, value, and foundation is to risk the life in our souls. If God can create the things that are from the things that are not, how do we set limits on what God may yet do? Can the uncertainty of our certainty lead to a grander vision? What is revealed if we choose not to return to our old ways and expand our love in our interim? If, as followers of Jesus, we believe that he did not leave us bereft of hope, that in his last act of generosity he left us the spirit to see in a way the world cannot see, then, at the very least, we possess the tools to shout against those afflicted with certainty, those bound by the brokenness of hand-me-down stories and living oppressive faith lives.

As I feel my way through the darkness of my faith walk, however, I know I would just as soon avoid people like Nora Pryn. I can't pretend that if I bump into raging fundamentalists in the darkness, I will even consider inviting them to walk with me toward a different light. In my better moments, I think I want to consider reconciliation, but failure has always been my companion, presenting to me my most disabling memories. It is not the acknowledgement of my failure, however, that is so pronounced and defeating, it is after I confess and then live as if I would do it again.

Chapter Sixteen

Hypocrisy Has Its Merits

A brother once asked Sisoes the Great: "Father, what can I do? I have fallen into sin." The Staretz answered: "Rise again." The brother said, "I rose and fell." The Staretz answered: "Rise again." The brother answered: "How often must I fall and rise up?" The Startetz said: "Until your death." Ignatius Byranchaninov, Ordinary Graces

When David died, he deprived me of an absorbing occupation: wondering what delicate principle kept him alive. Late in June, he gave up walking the neighborhood, relenting finally to the insistence of loving friends, but not without silent protestations. There must be neighborhoods in the world where David would not have attracted attention, but Seneca was not one of them. A lanky white gay man wearing a skull cap in summer, striding like a circus performer on stilts was odd, even by David's lack of fashion standards. He plodded more by vague hints of wonder than any consideration of physical purpose; he set his gait more by intuition and appeared happily content to serve as both a humorous and despised piece of gossip to neighbors peering out curtain-less windows.

"My brain seems to be asleep," he shared one Tuesday. "It's stopped sending me signals to inhale deeply. I pant like a dog after a summer run. I can barely make the forty steps to the back of the church now."

He lay in his bed most of the day; he was so dependent on what people did for him that had his conversation not been so contemplative, one might have thought he was blind. He smelled of death, but he had not yet seen enough of the one person in the world in whom he was most interested, himself.

For three years, David shared that he suspected a different happiness was waiting for him. But now, after these years, I wonder if maybe it was a part of him all the time, that the life he thought he might like to live was the one he was already living. Death bullied him, demanding his full participation, but he never relented in his belief that he could still be more than what others ascribed for him. Fear and doubt, but also exhilaration, played regularly on the gymboree that was his mind. He rearranged his life. He was a son, friend, lover, seeker, and I knew him as a gentle, relentless, and consistent heretic.

"No one but Jesus has a clue as to which end is up. I can't name one person. I mean, who understands really that we lug the kingdom of God around in our bones. I can't see it. People mumble the Lord's Prayer as nothing more than a chorus. If you don't see Jesus for who he was, what's the point of praying the prayer?" he said. "Worse, so many people seem confident in their stupidity and sentimentality. You have to be God's child to know that. Your profession, pastor, is filled with mercenaries, men and women who manipulate, distort, making Jesus some impotent version of St. Francis. Gotta make Jesus more loveable, someone easily dismissed. Maybe Jesus took right and wrong too seriously; maybe he distanced himself from the world a little too much, but for all of his quirks, he was superior to these quacks who only embrace him to line their pockets. A lot of crooks and few geniuses in your profession. And you have to somehow make peace with that. If I were you, I would be embarrassed."

During the last weeks, he moved his engravings of altar pictures and his candle cluster from his living room into his bedroom. He gazed at them with the eye of a watchful parent, attending to other practical duties, but always aware of something bigger, even better, symbolized by the light. He embraced the suggestiveness of the objects and their carnival promise that a spiritual visitation was always possible without question. "Even I am entitled to a low-grade, crass spiritual advisor, don't you think?" he shared repeatedly when any one pressed him to talk about his obsession.

He fumbled with one of his seven rosaries, wearing at least one each day as a charm bracelet to ward off fear. He preferred rubbing the beads, rolling them around, across, and through his fingers, to beating the hell out of his pillow in frustration and anger.

"I've been reading Camus," he shared almost nonchalantly as he stumbled toward the bathroom.

"You read Camus in the bathroom?" I shouted.

"Nobody reads Camus in the bathroom," he laughed, "but I've decided he's my go-to existentialist. I picked it up the other day and said why not. I have a bookshelf full of books given to me by well-meaning people. Each book assumes too much, writers wanting to help me die with whatever peace looks like to them. People drop by books that give the impression death can be taught some manners. Are they suggesting that I might learn how to die at my convenience? That's bullshit. How many self-help books on dying are out there? Dear God of all that is holy, there's only one plot. Take the books, pastor, please. No one should get to write about dying except the person who gets resurrected. All those books get to the end too quickly, my end. Camus never gets to the end. The last chapter is just as depressing as the first."

"Interesting selection," I interrupted. "It would not have been my first choice if I was dying. I don't know if it would ever be a first choice."

"I know. I found the book in the kitchen behind the toaster. I must have put it on the counter when I moved in. I remember reading it when I lived in the city. It must have gotten thrown into the utensil box," he said, melting into his bed, a puddle of sweat and fierce aroma.

"I have two questions: You haven't moved your toaster in three years? Haven't wiped the counter down? Bread crumbs, bagel crumbs? I have a question about Camus, but my mind keeps going to the colony of bugs building hideouts with no fear of reprisal on top of your Formica."

"I don't use the toaster," he said. "It has its place. It fits neatly in the corner. I have everything a normal kitchen is supposed to have. I just don't use everything," he continued.

"Except as cover for books, right? A shield?"

"Why are you giving me shit about a toaster," he said, turning toward me with the commitment of a slug.

"It's not about the toaster. It's about Evie and Camille knowing you haven't wiped down your counter in three years. If I tell them that, you know what is going to happen. They will gather in Hazmet suits and scrub the kitchen. Then, my friend, they will look at your living room. Might as well pick up and clean in there. And then, dear David, they will come for you. All your piles will be sorted as essentials and non-essentials. You won't be able to find anything. The notes you write, the prayers you jot down, gone. Dear God, clean your kitchen! I don't want to have a meeting with them to discuss sanitizing your apartment. It doesn't have the punch of Camus, but it's practical. And just to be clear, you won't find the meaning of life in Camus. I read it in seminary; it was required reading for a preaching seminar I took."

"How does Camus help you be a preacher?" he said as he sloughed toward the door frame next to his bed.

"It doesn't, except to direct you to real harshness, that scent of harshness that a writer like Camus offers anyone who might find comfort that their shit is manageable. People read Camus to share at parties, that while my life, your life, is hard, only Camus can take you where you don't want to go—considering the meaningless of all of life. The professor wanted us to read books that deal with the issues people face—loss, indifference to life, hopelessness. What he didn't tell us is people get tired of that shit quickly. No one can survive the choices Camus presents."

"That doesn't sound helpful at all," David said. "I don't need Camus to tell me that. Life plays out in shit most days and people deal with the smell in the only way handed down to them. I started reading <u>The Plague</u> to see if I am asking the right questions. I've never believed my dying can have any meaning except for those who watch me die. And all of you are parasites. I've decided my job is to feed you as long as I can. I told Jack that the other day. I think I offended him. I think I wanted to hurt him because he's so damn gallant. He keeps going. It feels like he's learned the answer to a secret I wish I knew, that he's guessed how the trick of this life works. He knows his duty, takes it where he finds it, even looks for it as much as possible. I need to apologize. He calls me Dave. No one calls me Dave, except Jack. And I don't know why but I like it. I know I can't disconnect from him emotionally, any of you. I don't have time to be offended. I have so few friends. I think about all of you as a wedding bouquet with all the same flowers. You smell of love."

"We don't need to be fond of you all the time to wish to stay connected with you," I shared. "I do think most of us are on guard around you; we consider too long how easily, without intention, we can offend you. You hold all the cards. Your emotions win every day. I hope you realize that?"

"That I can be an asshole?"

"You know each one of us. All of us are different, except in one thing. You get to play the lead in the story. We are secondary characters. There's no room for any emotions except yours. It's draining, David. You've got this private identity down. Good for you but this little snotty crusade you are living against everybody who gives a whit about you is tiring. It's starting to get a little rank, this stink of separation. And I can't pray it out of the room. And, yes, you can be an asshole, but I also feel we are close enough friends that I don't always think about you misunderstanding me. One of your gifts is you don't suspect us of insensitivity."

"I just want to feel alive by myself. I wonder if death has the power to push me forward toward each day's expectation. I live in the blackest of moments. Rarely does light shine through, but when it does, I want to notice it. Everyone needs a special room, pastor, where you can spend an hour or so unaware of what is going on, not worrying about what people will do for you or what you owe them. Maybe some magic will happen in the room, or nothing, but there is possibility. And pastor, I want you to know that I don't suspect any of you, but I do suspect most Christians," he shared looking at me with a rare intensity.

"I want the wilderness to serve as my teacher for reasons I am still unable to develop fully in my mind," he continued. "I can't explain my fascination with the desert. I am not afraid of dying of thirst, and I hope to leave before cramping. Its strength is its amorphous shape, revealing the oddest of perplexities and uncertainties—illusory projections about God, the glitter of appearances, and the strength of my hypocrisy. They are all idols that deflect from the naked experience of wonder without preconditions. And my secrets? I want them nearby. I should leave them behind buried in the sand of my rationalizations, but they are my most precious idols. What most people don't know is I have happy secrets, revealing just how far I have travelled in my faith journey, how much distance I have put between myself and my most fitful, debilitating pain. The wilderness asks very little except my secrets. My spiritual health depends on the sincerity of my hypocrisy."

Chapter Seventeen

Who Will Win the Memorial Service?

There is a wolf in me, fangs pointed for tearing gashes. There is a fox in me, I nose in the dark and take sleepers and eat them and hide the feathers. O, I am the keeper of the zoo."
Carl Sandburg, <u>Autumn Movement</u>

Ruth stood at the edge of David's casket, her finger delicately tracing an outline of her heart across what she considered his most beautiful feature, his hands. They rested tenderly on top of each other as a quiet prayer, an act of receiving, even blessing. She scanned his face with no thought of memorization but managed a side-long glance of his sunken cheeks, drawn as if he was holding his breath on a dare. A faint, almost pleasant odor emanated from the casket to cover the Lazarus stench of David being dead five days. His face, waxed and polished, doused with a grim makeup, looked unsure of any new revelations on the other side of the door. The rest of him behaved the way corpses do.

Ruth remembered a hundred trifles that she knew were now irrelevant, yet they weighed heavily on her spirit. Even now, they were trifles, she acknowledged, and what did she possess, if anything, that would help her understand them more graciously.

It came to her that she failed at something grand. She wanted to think of herself as David's protector, but she possessed no muscle and always let her words be her strength. She had written more than three letters to Nora Pryn, but David denied her permission to send them.

"Ruth, this is not going to end well for me," David had shared. "I've made my peace with that. You haven't, but then you haven't tried. Your beginning assumption is flawed. You are assuming my mother wants to change, or would change if presented with better facts. Daniel and I tried more than once to explain the science; homosexuality is not a choice. I have extended family who have tried as well. You want her to soften, and I wouldn't mind it, but she's gone. When people like my mother walk away from a relationship, they eventually slip behind some defensive wall to protect their beliefs. My mother knows if she removes one brick from her wall, the entire wall crumbles in her mind. And, Ruth, you don't know this, no reason you should, but she needs me dying the way I'm dying even more than I need any put-on reconciliation."

"Walls are dismantled one brick at a time. One brick, then another, more light each time. Eventually, she would see her son on the other side of the wall," Ruth shot back, perplexed at David that she had to make her case so forcefully.

"She's on the other side, shoring up the wall, Ruth. Look, be angry, roll your eyes, whatever you need, but find some room to pity her, too. This life isn't working for me. I can choose to die a thousand deaths each day when I think of my mother. Each hope for her is another fatal blow when I think of my fondest memory of her. I can die so many times each day, I forget I am dying. I'm now living for the only death that matters. This apartment reeks of ghosts. I prefer being haunted by dead ghosts, not a half-dead one like Nora. I know this will never satisfy you, but I want you to sleep at night after I'm gone. I know you. You are many things, Ruth, but I know if you don't like someone, you are done with them forever."

Ruth frowned, which she seemed to welcome as her go-to facial tick. She remembered one of her last conversations with David. "Why worry about those who have hurt you," she had said. "There is an excuse for them. They are assholes. You, on the other hand? There is no excuse," she teased.

"I need you to find an excuse for me," he smiled. "I've spent too much of my life trying to be perfect so God would love me, that God would have to love me because I was trying to do everything right. I once believed my mother's code of morality. Eventually, I learned I couldn't take it with me. Honestly, looking at where I am now, I wish I had never tried. The past twelve years I've been working so hard to stay alive, but now, now, I'm not afraid to rest. God knows who I am, even if my mother doesn't. And I don't have to impress God anymore."

Ruth returned to David's face, his five-day dead gray face, his head cradled on a taffeta pillow stuffed with memory foam, an expensive perk she thought excessive. She imagined how flat her hair would look, "splayed like a worn slipper" on such a cushion. She saw herself in the future as a dying woman without one of her most cherished memories. She was still alive, barely. Her cancer had not killed her yet; the treatment's efficacy always just short of healing.

Labeled a "perpetual" cancer patient, oncologists managed her symptoms but never issued a get-out-of- jail remission card to carry in her wallet. She lived her solitary life wanting to believe that the sensation of being alive was enough for her. There were fleeting moments when she thought she could model it for others. She also wondered, now that David was dead, if life for her would be better. She argued with herself that it was because there is love. Death is also good, she reasoned, but there is no love.

Ruth was innately suspicious of the Pryns and their tribe, but she was wary of most people. Even as David's stature in the eyes of many within the congregation and the community increased, she felt cold, "damp of spirit," that some in the sanctuary that afternoon saddled their prejudice to the perversity that David was small. She recoiled, shuddered at the thought of them mocking him: "Poor little David has become the hero of their tragedy," she imagined them saying as they huddled in their corner of the sanctuary. She glared at them effectively; she felt on her lips the taste of dishonor. She knew that if she had chosen to speak to them, she would have cursed.

A woman gingerly approached Ruth's shadow, standing behind her like a wounded animal with nothing to lose worth keeping. Few people in the sanctuary took note of her presence around the casket. No one knew that her immeasurable grandeur was buried beneath her outward appearance of pastels and pleats.

She had entered the sanctuary before noon, just as the doors to the church opened for the memorial. She followed a woman pulling herself up the stairs, the woman's hands clutching the railing like a vise. She paused at the portal at the top of the stairs; she hesitated to the point of inertia, as tentative as a part-time atheist considering the merits of blasphemy if she walked on existing graves. She took a step and tripped, the heel of her loafer brushing against the threshold that separated the staircase from the narthex. As she fell, she looked heavy and out of control. Her more than modest weight squandered any hint of dexterity. She flailed and grasped the air for directions. Eventually, gravity forced her nose to kiss the knee of a young man holding court with some of David's friends from the city. A young woman, dressed substantially, stood at that irritating distance between having to assist and being judged for indecision.

The fall bloodied her lip the way one bites one's tongue carelessly chewing pork. Her cheek reddened instantly, having scraped the seam of the young man's Levis. "Are you all right?" the young man asked, lifting her head to a more reasonable angle, the cup of his hand serving as a bowl.

"I'm fine," she said, immediately flippant and off putting. She got to her knees as quickly and as painfully as an aging priest rising from his morning prayers.

"I know we all have to die," she spouted defiantly, "but I thought my death might be grander than breaking my neck in a church." She repositioned her much-too-colorful blouse and pressed the wrinkles from her skirt. She was a woman not afraid of dying; living was the greater hell.

She composed herself enough to manage the long aisle, wobbling from one finial to the next as if trying to zig-zag from stray bullets. She stopped at one point and sat on the edge of the cushion, bracing her hands on the pew in front. She waited for an appropriate time to approach the casket, unaware there was never a right time approach Ruth. She brushed against Ruth's shoulder as she side-stepped around her to get a frontal view. "David was always kind to me," she mumbled, almost as an aside, soft enough for Ruth to hear but not to take notice.

"He was kind to everybody," Ruth replied, her eyes still fixated on David's body, which she thought had contracted an inch or so since the funeral director rolled the casket from the back steps.

"You didn't hear me," the woman repeated with emphasis, her stress not on the words but the sentiment, the way insistence becomes the only necessary prompt. "I said he was nice to me. I don't give a shit if he was nice to others. He was nice to me."

Ruth turned toward her. She recognized her face. She knew her only as an exception, a peripheral part of the guests on Tuesday nights, but at that moment the woman had worked her way beyond a cliché.

"David let me take meals home to my family," she continued. "I didn't have to sit with anyone at the church. I didn't have to sign in or take a number. I didn't have to be served. He wrapped the meal for me. He knew my situation. He asked about me, but never pressed me for details, except to ask if I was safe. I came today because I wanted him to know I imagined myself sitting down to a meal I wasn't responsible for, reserved just for me. I know there are people like me; I'm just glad David knew about me. I like the table setting by the casket. I can't imagine many people making the connection, but I like it. A meal feels so important. I am here because he knew he would never share it with me, but I wanted him to know he did. I wanted him to know that. I know he can't hear me, but I felt like I needed to say it aloud to someone."

"Will you stay for the service?" Ruth asked.

"No, I've only got a few minutes away from the house. I don't do church anyway. There's nothing some preacher can tell me that I don't already know about David. I know what I need to know."

No chapter of Covenant's past was more perfectly recorded than its story with David. At times we were more zoo than sanctuary, our fangs bared. We circled menacingly around those who lived to take our weak. The angry lion was often dominant; we tore at others, trying to protect David's dying. We were unapologetically dogmatic about inclusion, clearing up, as we reasoned, the issue that the church beyond our confines had been bungling for years. It might be said we were ruining faith for people. Fair enough. Jesus warned that we could never be naïve about peace, especially manufactured peace. He said we would be at each other's throats until the end. And that's the way it played out during the memorial.

"What is the poetry of this moment?" Ann shared with me the day of the service. "I think we supposed to leave behind something beautiful. We know the other side will not do their part. The best that they can do is get inside our heads."

"They've been living there for too long, "I shared. "I feel as comfortable as I need to be right now. I think I want to be gracious, but, Ann, tell me how I do that while biting my tongue. It's not easy speaking with a mouthful of blood."

"Just try and not make the service meaningless and sad. Share God's love and sit down," she said, missing that one significant piece that everyone gathered was looking through the wrong end of God's telescope.

We had little to offer David the day of his memorial service except to provide an opposing view. David had begun to live in his memories, exploring in his mind and heart everything that he missed in his life, and resting sadly content that his life had peaked too early. Each daydream that involves the past is a ticket to the grave. Yet, what did this neglected son have to look forward to? We tamped down what anger we had toward God who had sentenced our friend to die against his wishes. We thought placidly about the need for church reform; we decried why death is a consequence of birth. In the end, we decided to bless him, that love's solemn function is to make a loved one unique and irreplaceable.

To invoke such a blessing required corporate voices, the testimonies of those who ministered to David for three years. If a blessing were to be invoked, it had to be the vocation of more than just paid staff. The power of blessing is deep-boned. People spend their whole lives waiting for a blessing from a father or mother. Our concern was not the fact that David, who spent his final years trying to rewrite his story, wanted a blessing, his parents' blessing. We knew it would not come, but we still grieved that it was never offered.

On that last day, we asked for God's blessing on our friend because we did not have enough good words to offer ourselves. We took comfort in knowing that all blessing words are borrowed words. We confessed that we did not have enough good words to offer because of the remnants of how David's memory was distorted and inexorably linked to our fragile spirits. We fell back on what we hoped was grace; we asked God to bless because to ask God for a blessing is to borrow the power of God to forgive.

Sometimes we are given a privileged glimpse of God's grace, not because we understand it or have any claim on it, but because we have become a channel for it. Somehow the act of blessing puts us in a place where God draws near and takes up residence in our hearts. I wondered if it were possible for God to touch such a moment, touching not only David, but us? And the Pryns as well.

After the service, we gathered at the Northeast corner of the cemetery, notable for little else except it was named in honor of Dan Emmett, the author of the Confederate tune, "Dixie." At the entrance, a soldier's monument faces South, which I can only assume is his heart's direction. Wrens and robins kept circling and plunging at the taillights of the hearse. The grounds, still divided between Protestants and Catholics, felt more embarrassing than exclusive. David had finagled his way into the Catholic section without any reference letters, only his crooked smile to influence.

The funeral directors pushed and prodded and goaded five other young men to carry the casket thirty feet from the hearse to the gravesite. Peter Pryn was summoned, but he refused. He possessed a great dislike to being counted on, almost claiming an irresistible need of disappointing.

Nora Pryn positioned herself near the head of the casket and consigned her son to earth. She stood at the edge of the grave but not close enough to fall in or be pushed. She peered into the deep and smelled sulfur. It was a solemn time, but strangely it was not heavy. There was a freedom from the oddities of the sanctuary, the performance, the choosing of sides. Outside there appeared a certain geniality of things. If it was sad to think of David, it was not too sad, since death had had no violence for him. He had been dying so long; he was so ready. Everything had been expected and prepared. I saw tears in the eyes of church people, but they were not tears that blinded. I looked around at the beauty of the day, the splendor of nature, the sweetness of the plot where they placed him, and the bowed heads of good friends.

Nora Pryn looked the way people look when someone else dies. It happens to other people. Death was disagreeable, but it was her son's death, not her own. To her credit, she had never flattered herself that her own death would be unpleasant to anyone. The worst part of dying in her mind was it exposed one to be taken advantage of.

I sense there will always be people who seek to defeat death with the spiritual weapons their minds have invented. Because they fight with nothing but words, pronounced sacred after their late inception, there can be no advance in the area of heart and soul. And I confess I let myself wonder if true immortality will be denied them.

I can't remember what I shared at the grave. I pray I did not drone on, trying to convince every moss-backed headstone in the cemetery of David's contribution to the practical theory that love changes everything. Ghosts have little to offer except short-term thrills. In the long run, they prove to be exceedingly dull. I hope I didn't pray that people reconsider. It was not that kind of reunion. The gold-dust twins, Christianity and insistence, had set up their own Vanna White Wheel of Fortune around a pile of dirt. In some perfunctory expression of hope, I considered spinning one last time for reconciliation but ended up bankrupt and disappointed.

The shallowness around David's grave was palpable. To some, his life was expressly a system of rewards and punishments. They missed that the payment for the triumph of belief, or any victory over doubt, created as many problems as their witch hunts. I wonder if most deaths are suicides, people who lack curiosity about life, finding stringy joy in existence, and are all too willing to cooperate with disease, accident, and violence. Death seems content to best us even as we live. David's antagonists reveled in unhappiness, and when one is unhappy, one gets to take oneself seriously. Unhappiness may be the ultimate form of self-indulgence.

I hope I presented David as a glorious man. It's a lazy conclusion. His constant prattle about the meaning of life and God made me tired. On his most vital days, David included enough displeasure at his dying to displease those of us who ministered to him daily that the church was actually without representation. There were times when he needed help, but God was in a meeting when he rang. He persisted. There was a humility in his listening, and his response was always something more genuine than his preconditions. There was a curious aroma around his life. I found it increasingly difficult to pinpoint its presence, but it lifted my spirits in a shy way, fostering the secret hope that some blessed encounter waited in the next room.

Early in the year of his death, David wrote an article for the local newspaper promoting our Hot Meals' ministry. "It's more than a food program," he wrote. "It's a ministry of love and compassion. The meals are for those hungry—not just for food, but hungry for fellowship, for conversation, for love. If your stomach is growling or your heart is aching, come and be fed. I've consistently made an error when tabulating the number of guests each Tuesday. Instead of a weekly average of forty-three folks, it is more open-ended. Weekly average? One or more. There is always room for more, including God."

    David taught me a few things. He was frustratingly realistic. He was also grateful for any small wonder that wormed its way into his death vigil. To recognize any small wonder qualifies one to imagine something even grander.

Epilogue

Resolution is Often Solitary

And you expect us to manage our wilderness with smiles? You expect us to revisit our desert hangouts and dark places more than once? How do I plan for that? For more than a day? Even the prospect of resurrection feels like too much to ask. David Arthur Pryn

We each get a ticket to tour this unpredictable life. If our life is dull, the sentence is wistfulness. If it is interesting, too, we forge relationships and interact with fellow travelers. However we choose to let this one and precious life play out, a scripted ending awaits us: There is an end. It is impending, clearly visible each day behind the sheer draperies of our lives. And it shapes most of what we attempt or avoid.

David died as separate from his parents as the day they dropped him off in the city as a teenager. Moral insistence, so ingrained in them, polluted every neuron of their brains. They created in their minds and hearts hymns of ritualized brutality. Having a fling with "messiahood" will do that to you. Peter and Nora Pryn imagined only a fiery finish for their son and appeared to look forward to it.

David experienced the wilderness on two fronts. He knew wilderness first as isolation-- cut off emotionally from his family and driven into the desert because of his single violation of how to live as a sexual being. He lived and died in a war zone, a target of spiritual snipers, loading and re-loading, as necessary. The sword of death hung precariously over his life for ten years. At twenty-one, he wrote that "tonight my most dreaded fear was confirmed as a reality. It is a fear greater than fear itself. Actually, it is even worse than the fear of death. It is the fear of dying. I am…HIV positive."

Harsh realities were not his only realities, however. To a certain extent, with the proper energy and perspective, one chooses how one wishes to live. David also knew the wilderness as possibility, as a prompt inching him toward an intimacy beyond the strictures of faith rules first presented to him. He didn't think long about any abstract rightness. He happened upon a purposeful life with better friends, women and men who encouraged his soul's constant movement, and asking he set for himself unattainable goals they knew he would never achieve.

We watched David fight for his best cause, picturing God in a better light. He did not push for a future with God or even let his mind rest in his next eternity for any length of time. Too much yearning for the future was as anti-life as dwelling too long in the past. The apostle Paul found it necessary to name love as the winner of the "greatest of these" contest. I wonder if a recount is in order because I witnessed David's pronounced sense of hope that won out over resignation. It served as the one virtue that kept him occupied from constantly listening for death loitering outside his apartment and trying to slip past the doorman.

David possessed a fine mind and, with proper training, would have made a serviceable theologian. I didn't judge him about his understanding of prayer, or his Pooh-like picture of God walking side by side with him through difficult days offering counsel with a dollop of honey. He fuzzed over too many items of doctrine for my taste. His theology was grounded in lived experience, and God was only experienced connection best expressed with new friends.

Engaged spirituality can be as frightening as any imagined fear when reflecting on one's worst life. It is movement from what appears as bleakest black to most luminous and everything in between. David did not wither completely as he lived the revelation. He and I tried kindness. We professed kindness to each other, spooned in larger doses as our relationship matured. But even kindness is often exposed as impotent in the face of what humans are capable of. Witnessing the horror show of a cruel heart in action is devastating; to see another heart turn cold and hard in the face of suffering inflicted, or, worse, to see a heart revel at suffering is a hellish vision.

I wanted instinctively to deny it and unsee it. After these years, it's all I see, even want to see. There is a part of me that refuses to let go of those memories because to do so is a betrayal of David's suffering. I also confess, these ten years after David's death, that I exhibited such cruelty, that such cruelty may have been residing in my soul all along, and, I, in my complacency, failed to recognize it. I remember how easily I am prone to hypocrisy as well. Growing up, I was told so often I was a sinful wretch and rotten to the core from the day I was born, that for a time I considered myself the anti-Christ.

I don't remember my early teachers encouraging me to seek wilderness experiences and their accompanying strength. I have spent most of my life and too much time and money attending conferences taking notes on how to stay out of them. I don't know anyone who succeeds in the wilderness entirely or forever. If I did, I am not sure I would want to reach out to them as potential friends. Still, I find the desert appealing, so much so that I might consider a timeshare. The cactus, the most arrogant of succulents, humming defiance that it could survive nuclear winter, believes that presumptuous. Admittedly, while I lean toward faith strength found in barren places, I also sense I can only manage the dues and fees for short periods. There are too many times my search for God or any scintilla of faith feels cost prohibitive. There are too many times I have buyer's remorse.

Still, the wilderness is where I want to inventory my spiritual life. It is there I unmask and where I ask where I intend to give my attention. I find comfort in sagebrush spirituality, my faith flitting and flaring with each wind gust, and me unable to pin anything down with certainty. In the desert, I face my biases, my antipathy toward those who harm in God's name, and refute the temptation to make faith an ideal. I learn, again, that if I want to destroy a relationship, then all that is needed is me bringing to that relationship what I think it should be. In that way, I am as guilty as the Pryns.

Mystics speak of two faith paths: The Via Positiva and Via Negativa, both parts of one bigger path. On the positive path, I use all the words, images, experiences, and ideas I have about God that help me know something, anything really, of God. My words and ideas, always as fragile as stained glass, become a first window open to the divine. There is also the second path, the negative path, the path of not-knowing. On this path, I have to let go of those same images and experiences of God that felt complete at the time but are now no longer appropriate. I must face what I do not know; I must travel in silence, without sight, and beyond beliefs. I confess I have rarely chosen this path. Most of the time, the path has been thrust upon me. In the words of poet John Keats, it is the path of "negative capability" where I must choose to live in uncertainties, mysteries without "any irritable reaching after fact and reason."

In the dark of the desert night, fierce and fiery as it is unrelenting, the veils of my delusions are torn and burned. There my heart is purified of its vile lust and other impurities. I can no longer betray what I know has sustained my soul for too long. It was in the dark that I named my fear for David and where it might lead. I know myself well enough that my go-to position is not trust but suspicion when faced with fierce faith circumstances. I repeatedly failed to see how frequent my disappointment with God surfaced and how easily I returned to faith as a crassly transactional enterprise: "God, show your stuff. Rescue David. I am not asking for his physical healing, but a smattering of spiritual wealth sprinkled around his neighborhood. I will try and do my part, God, but you had better do yours in return."

Faith and anger live side by side in my heart when I think of David's enemies. Does faith have any effect on anger that resides so comfortably in my skin? Can faith help anger move on and through and out and not set up lodging? "Resist no thoughts" is the first principle of centering prayer. Do not resist them; resistance is futile. I confess I have expended too much energy trying to keep them out. The desert prompts such introspection. A second principle is "retain no thoughts," which has proven to be the most difficult of instructions when I think of how David died, absent from any hint of love and embrace. I want to let them float by like barges on the Green River near my birth home; I want them to float in and float out. The desert presents such a possibility. I can have my anger, but do not have to be anger. It has a place, a temporary place, if you consider ten years temporary, but anger does not have to rule.

The desert meets me when I think I would choose, if pressed, to give up this vocation, surrender, cede my beliefs, observing in fear that the prevailing religions of the world contain little of what I love. Not meeting any standard of simple decency and kindness, but only that of spiritual violence forged in the furnace of fear, hate, and exclusion resides in my soul. I desire to placate my mood, especially in those times of self-pity when I contemplate how ineffective I've been teasing a bigger picture of God: an alternative to the prevailing spiritual violence, violence that is not only episodic, as expressed in these pages, but egregious, the result of a violent belief system, institutionalized, championed and defended by strict interpretations of sacred texts.

I assume that this could sound like bad news for many, but I don't think it is. I believe it is good news—because even if no one ever wants to go there, and even if those of us who end up there want out again as soon as possible, the wilderness is still one of the most reality-based, spirit-filled, life-changing places a person can be. I do want to give up at times. I can't because of God, that spark that ignites my spirit's fire on the dampest of faith days. I have learned that faith cannot open a door that is not there, but, in the desert, I also know that faith can open a door that the human eye cannot see. So, I continue to walk by faith and not by the awful, disturbing sights of this world, trusting in the goodness of God to do all God can do while also asking me to partner with God to do all that is possible.

I continue to stare into the darkness in front of me; I formulate a visit schedule, purchase an entry ticket, and move in without luggage, realistic that the desert's benefits and affections, when measured against what I've have always known as light, may leave me wanting. If I want everything to be about the light, then my preoccupation will lead to a kind of frailty and false perception.

After Jesus' baptism, Jesus, being Jesus, intentionally walks into a desert to be tested, which is not entirely accurate. The story goes that the Spirit led him to be tested, which carries its own theological baggage about God's surface goodness. I interpret that his being "led by the spirit" means Jesus didn't put up much of a fight or complain too loudly or forcefully.

Apparently, Jesus sensed the merits of the desert, its fascinations. Not one of us, however, is likely to be put to the same test. When it's our turn, none of us is going to get the

"Jesus" test. We're going to get the regular old Adam and Eve test, which means that the devil won't need much more than an all-you-can-eat buffet and a tax refund to turn our heads.

The wilderness freed Jesus from all the devilish attempts to distract him from his true purpose, from a hungry craving for things with no power to give him life, from any illusion he might have had that God would make his choices for him. After forty days in the wilderness, Jesus had not only learned to manage his appetites, he had also learned to trust the Spirit that had led him there to lead him out again, presumably with the kind of clarity and grit he could not have found anywhere else.

Science reveals that trees communicate with each other. A stately elm attacked by "boring" enemies will transmit a warning to other trees in the forest so they can commence manufacturing a chemical designed specifically to repel that particular variety of bug. Reports from the infested tree allow other trees to protect themselves. This information, scientists posit, is likely broadcast as aroma.

The mission of Jesus was at least preparing our olfactory senses for a different odor. Instead of swords and knives, as well as other weapons of spiritual violence—arrogance, fear, the bricks and mortar of certainty--he asked we consider the faint hint of jasmine. This Jesus, whose commandment "love your enemies" has proven too strong a dosage to swallow, will not relinquish the command or cede it to hermetic malcontents taking up residence in God's multiple deserts.

I can't help but wonder, as I think of David, if Jesus came into the world to deliver us from evil, but rather to deliver us from our evil intent. Any good versus evil dichotomy always feels forced. Our culpability is pronounced, and those who desire to follow the way of Jesus need the kind of clarity and grit found only in the wilderness. If we spend a lot of time and money trying to acquire whatever it takes to grow our soul without seeing new buds, then maybe a little spell in the wilderness is worth a try—a few weeks of choosing to live on less, not more—of practicing subtraction instead of addition, not because our regular life is bad but because we need to make sure it is our life—the one we long to be living—which can be hard to do when we are living on spiritual junk food and grudges.

Experiencing the wilderness is discovering what life is like without the usual painkillers. In the desert we learn what led us to use them in the first place; we acknowledge the signs of things gone badly wrong, the pacifiers that soothe our fears. After we have reached for our pacifier a few times and remembered it's not there—not because someone stole it from us but because we made a conscious decision to give it up—then we may discover a whole new level of conversation with ourselves and God.

Society will tell us that losing our pacifiers will kill us, but it's rarely true. All that's going to happen is that we're going to suck air for a while, then we're going to hiccup, then we're going to look around and see things without that pink plastic circle under our noses, which is going to turn out to be a good thing both for us and for everyone else in our lives.

It would be a mistake for me to try and describe someone else's wilderness test. Only they can do that because only they know what devils have their number and what kinds of bribes they use to get them to pick up. Still, we've all been there—a hospital waiting room, a parking lot where you couldn't find your car on the day you lost your job. It may have been the kind of wilderness in the middle of our chest when we begged for a word from God and heard nothing but the wheezing bellows of our breath.

All I can say is that a voluntary trip to the desert is a great way to practice getting free of those devils for life. It is where we lose our appetite for things that cannot save us; it is where we learn to trust the Spirit that led us there to lead us out again, ready to worship the Lord your God and serve no other all the days of our life.

Wildernesses come in so many shapes and sizes that the only way we can tell we are in one is to look around for what we normally count on to save our life and come up empty. No food. No earthly power. No special protection—just a Bible-quoting devil and a whole bunch of sand.

Sooner or later, every one of us will get to sit for our wilderness test, our trip to the desert to discover who we really are and what our lives are about. Thank you, my friend, dear David, who walked with me on mine.

Made in the USA
Columbia, SC
30 June 2021